HOME FIRES
THE LONG ROAD HOME

CAT JOHNSON

PROLOGUE

Prudence Swenson stood at the window on the highest floor of the massive house and watched the long line of cars arriving via the driveway down below.

Each one stopped by the front entrance. The guests inside, decked out in their finest black attire, got out and made their way to the front door while the valets, hired for the day, sped away to park the vehicle before returning to do it all again for the next arrival.

This was a popular event. People had turned out *en masse*. Meanwhile, she hid in what was now her bedroom, unable, or perhaps just unwilling to go downstairs. At least not quite yet. Maybe not at all.

Why should she go down and join all the strangers?

Who would miss her if she didn't? They were there to be seen, not to see her.

She had the Swenson name, but none of the power or prestige and sadly, none of the vast amounts of family wealth either.

That was the fate of the stepchild of a cousin, now orphaned and taken in by the good graces of the almighty Swenson family.

A wave of guilt hit her at the thought.

She shouldn't think like that. Myra, as she was allowed to call the woman who was technically her great-step-aunt—or was it step great-aunt—was sweet.

More accurately, Myra was shrewd, cunning and tough as nails, but she did have a kind side for family. And although there were those among the Swensons who had never considered Prudence family, Myra was not one of them.

Neither was Cadence, Myra's granddaughter. Similar in age, and therefore sharing a lot of interests growing up, they'd been friends since they'd both been eight. They still were, friends, although not as close as they'd been before.

There was a distance between them—literally and figuratively—after Cadence was sent away to the best boarding school in the country at age fifteen, while Pru continued to attend public school locally. As poor relations should, she supposed. Just as she supposed she should feel lucky she'd been stashed away in the attic bedroom and wasn't living on the streets now…

Her single mother marrying a Swenson—even one of the lesser family members—had been scandalous.

Her mother had been a factory worker. He was one of the big bosses. But they had fallen in love and, to the despair of some members of his family, Guy Swenson had married her mother. At eight, Pru had officially been adopted into the family. Guy had given her his last name and, like it or not, added her and her mom to the illustrious Swenson family tree.

Life was good for a while. For ten years the three of them—Guy, Pru and her mom—lived as a happy family in one of the four houses on the Swenson estate. Not in the "big house", meaning the brick 1910 mansion, complete with a ballroom on the third floor.

Instead, they'd lived in the Tudor-style guest house, which wasn't exactly roughing it. Compared to the tiny Albany apartment where she and her mother had shared a bed, the three-bedroom guest house was a castle.

Having her own room for the first time was

heaven. Living skipping distance away from her new best friend had been the stuff of dreams. Not to mention Cadence's gorgeous older brother Cal, the man she planned to marry one day…in her dreams.

That was all before Cadence went away to school and Cal Junior joined the military.

And before the crash. Or *the incident* as everyone referred to it within earshot of her.

A rainstorm, a slick highway and an out-of-control tractor trailer had wiped out her family and her happiness all at once.

She became an orphan the week she turned eighteen. Happy birthday to her.

The day after the accident, Myra had moved her into the main house. It was clear Calvin senior expected Pru to be grateful for his allowing her to move in at Myra's request. She supposed she was—as grateful as she could be at the moment.

She was eighteen now. They could have turned her out onto the street with her modest inheritance that Guy, never considering his own tenuous mortality, had put in a trust that couldn't be touched until she turned twenty-five.

So the Swensons had put her in what had once been servants' rooms, stuck under the eaves of the third floor. Not to be cruel—it was less like Cinderella than it sounded in spite of the similarities—but because the "big house" only had five bedrooms.

Apparently, ballrooms and open center hall staircases took up a lot of space. Myra, Cadence, Cal Junior, and Calvin Senior all had their own bedrooms on the second floor. And even though Cal was in California in the Navy, Myra was ever hopeful. She kept his room just as he'd left it, like a shrine, waiting for his return.

That made two of them who were waiting for Cal's homecoming...

Pru had opportunity to sneak into Cal's room only a couple of times over the past years since he'd left and Cadence had been sent away. While inside, ever vigilant as she listened for the sound of footsteps on the stairs, she'd run her finger over the framed pictures around the room. Or bury her face in the clothes he'd left in the closet—mostly suits which he wouldn't need now that he wore a uniform. All in hopes of getting a whiff of the scent of him, for lack of anything else from the boy—now man—whom she loved.

He was six and a half years older than she was. That half a year seemed very important. As a girl with a crush on her best friend's much older brother, her kind-of, sort-of but not really distant cousin, Pru preferred to think they were six and a half years apart rather than seven.

As if he'd ever be interested in her, no matter what the age difference. To him, she was his little sister's shadow. Nothing more. But a girl could hope. And because of that, she was happy to take the small third-floor bedroom if it meant Cal might be coming home soon to resume living in his larger one, a floor below.

So Pru had spent the last four days since the accident in her attic room with the sloped ceiling and window to the world going on below, waiting for time to pass. There, but not really there. Like a ghost. Probably not the only one, judging by the creaks and groans she heard while lying in bed sleepless at night.

She'd try to eat when they called her down to the grand dining room for meals. She'd turn off the light and lie awake when it was time to go to bed. She'd rise in the morning and put on whatever clothes her hand hit in the closet the house staff had stuffed full of her things from home—or rather the house on the property that used to be her home.

Besides the loss of her parents, which still seemed like a nightmare she'd wake from once she finally could fall to sleep, with Cadence and Cal Junior gone, she was the only young person in the oversized museum of a house. She lived there with an old lady, a slightly younger but still old man, and the staff, who were polite but not exactly friendly. Certainly not her friends.

Cadence was getting the best education money could buy, at a school which cost more per semester than Pru's mother had earned in a year on the Swenson's factory floor back when she'd been employed by the family before becoming one of them and quitting that job.

Pru was lonely, but she wasn't jealous. Not at all.

Remaining in the Albany suburb of Coeymans to finish her senior year of high school was fine with her. Preferable, actually. And she was just as happy to be attending SUNY Albany next year while Cadence would be at Wharton in Philly.

Coeymans was an affluent area and the public school system, supported by all those tax dollars from the mansions along the Hudson River, was good, as was the state university system in New York. Besides, the great divide between her and the Swenson family members who'd taken her in was already glaringly wide. She didn't need to be the charity case among the fancy, rich prep school kids in Cadence's school as well.

As the literal red-headed stepchild, she stood out enough from the Nordic Swenson family with her brown eyes and dark auburn locks that made her look as if she'd been dipped headfirst into a vat of dark red paint. Or blood.

At least she wasn't the only black sheep in the Swenson family. Cal Junior also had that honor as the son who made Uncle Calvin's jaw clench whenever someone mentioned his name.

Bad boy. Rebel. Blonde-haired and blue-eyed, like the rest of his family, he was too good looking for his own good.

It might have been what made him so cocky. And made him the only family member with enough hubris to stand up to Uncle Calvin, shun the family wealth and legacy and leave. Never to return…

Until now.

Cal was home for the funerals. He'd arrived last night, looking as sullen as she felt. From the tension she sensed between him and his father during their first reunion in years, she had a feeling it wasn't the shadow of her parents' death that had Cal looking so dark.

The *buzz* of her cell phone made her glance down.

It was a text from Cadence, who was in the middle of a semester abroad. Unlike Cal, Cadence wasn't coming home for the funerals. Pru had never felt so alone in all of her life.

Cadence: How are you?

She stared at the words on the text, not really comprehending them or much of anything right now. The sight of the open caskets and the mortician's failed attempt at making her mom and Guy look normal still filled her brain. But she'd been at this grieving orphan thing for a few days now and it was becoming second nature.

Without thinking too much about it, she typed in a reply.

Pru: I'm fine

Cadence: So sorry I'm not there!!

Pru stared at the new text. At the double exclamation points in particular, wondering if that made it more or less sincere.

She tapped the message and marked it with a heart emoji, which seemed appropriate, then stared at her cell phone, seeing it with new eyes. And new concern.

It was on Guy's phone plan. What would happen to it now? What would happen to *her* now with no money of her own?

Those thoughts broke her. Broke something free inside and brought a deluge of tears to her eyes. Tears that had refused to come during the funeral service or the days leading up to it. But they sure came now.

Was she really crying over the impending loss of her cell phone service?

She wiped the wetness away with the back of her hand when she heard footsteps on the stairs. By the time she turned toward the door Cal was standing there. His over six-foot frame filling the opening, making the room feel even smaller than before.

"Oh. Shit. Sorry." He frowned as he swayed slightly.

It was then she noticed the bottle of booze dangling from his hand. It looked like one of Uncle Calvin's bottles from the living room bar.

"I didn't realize you were in here," he continued.

In spite of that, he moved inside and flopped his long body into the one chair in the room.

She couldn't help but notice he'd filled out in the years since he'd left. He was not only older, but he also seemed wider. Harder.

And he looked ridiculous with all his long limbs spilling out of the tiny, upholstered armchair that was covered in faded pink rosebud fabric.

"It's okay. This is my room now. I live here, since…" She let the sentence trail off.

Of all the times over the years she'd imagined Cal

being alone with her—envisioned him in her bedroom —it had not been like this.

The furrow in his brow deepened. "Yeah. Sorry about that—your parents."

"Thanks." The word came out as it had dozens of times at the funeral home this morning.

He looked around him. "They couldn't find a better room for you? This is basically the frigging attic. Boxes of Christmas ornaments used to be stored in here."

"It's fine." She shrugged. "I don't mind it, really. It's quiet," she added, realizing he deserved more since he was the only one to comment on the lesser quality of her lodging compared to the *family* bedrooms downstairs.

"That it is. Quiet." He let out a snort accompanied by a small smile. "That's why I come up here to hide. I never had company before."

She cringed. "Sorry—"

"Fuck that. Don't *you* be sorry. I mean, hell…" He shook his head. "I don't even know what to say to you. What to do."

She knew what she wanted him to do. She wanted him to wrap his arms around her. Hold her until she didn't feel alone. Kiss her until she somehow forgot the horror of the past week. Make love to her until she felt like a woman ready to face this world, instead of a scared child all alone.

Those thoughts brought a fresh flood of tears to her eyes.

He cursed under his breath when he saw them and pushed out of the chair. Coming to her, he pulled her against him.

Wrapped in his arms, she cried harder.

To his credit, Cal didn't run. Silent, strong, he just held her with her face pressed against the rock-hard muscles of his chest, until the sobs wracking her body subsided and her tears stopped soaking the front of his white dress shirt.

She pulled back and looked at the wet spot she'd left, thankful she hadn't bothered to put on make-up this morning. Or for the last few mornings.

"Wanna drink?" he asked, holding up the bottle he still held in one hand.

"No. Thanks."

He nodded as his gaze met and held hers. It was then that it hit her how very close he was. Just inches separated them.

Such a short distance between his lips and hers. She tilted her head up, just a bit. A subtle silent invitation that he didn't miss as his gaze fell to her mouth and his nostrils flared with his intake of breath.

His throat worked as he swallowed hard, then he raised his eyes. "I, uh, should go."

"You don't have to," she said quickly as he dropped his hold on her and took a step back.

A small, crooked smile accompanied his sniff. "Yeah, I do."

Then Cal was gone. And she was alone. Again.

CHAPTER ONE

As Cal Swenson Junior pushed the metal bar up and counted his twentieth rep, the door to the weight room crashed open.

"It's fucking hot out there," Mo declared as he let a blast of hot air into the room.

Sitting up, Cal leveled a stare on his teammate. "Of course, it's hot out there. We're on the Horn of Africa. What did you expect? San Diego weather?"

Mo screwed up his mouth and grunted then asked, "You done?" when he saw Cal stand.

Cal nodded before grabbing a towel and wiping down the weight bench where, in spite of the A/C, he'd left a sheen of sweat. "Just finished."

That answer earned him another scowl from Mo.

"Sorry. If I'd known you were heading over I would have waited," Cal apologized.

At that, as if on cue, both Mo and Cal's pagers sounded.

Mo's eyes flew wide as Cal drew in a breath, knowing what the simultaneous summons meant. Good thing he hadn't waited to work out or he wouldn't have been able to, just like Mo wasn't going to get to now.

"What the fuck? Three fucking days until we head home and we're getting spun up now? Can't Echo team take this one? They're already here, ready to rotate in," Mo grumbled.

"Guess not," Cal answered as he followed Mo out the door where a blast of hot air immediately slapped him in the face.

Ignoring the sensation of being inside a pizza oven, they strode fast toward the building that held the war room. When they arrived he saw members of Alpha team already there and seated.

Cal lowered his six-foot two-inch frame into the vacant seat next to Slim and asked, "You know anything about this?"

Slim shook his head. "Not a damn thing."

As Cal glanced around the room, he realized the Echo team commander was there, as well as his own team's commander and the logistics personnel.

Something was up.

Lieutenant Commander Smyth moving to the front of the room, his expression grave, reinforced that theory. So did his flipping on the projector that displayed a map showing Ukraine and Russia.

Hound Dog, seated on the other side of Cal, let out a long low whistle at the sight.

Across the table, Mo rubbed his hands together as he said, "About damn time."

Apparently Mo's concern about an op just days before they were scheduled to head back to Coronado was forgotten at the prospect of finally getting into this fight they had, to date, been kept out of.

Smyth began, "Security video shows a troop of Russian soldiers have massacred two unarmed Ukrainian civilians, shooting them in the back inside a private office building located here."

The LT tapped the dot on the map to indicate the city as Hound Dog mumbled, "Bastards."

Slim agreed with a soft, "Those fucking war criminals are the ones who need to be shot."

"Understandably, civilians are now being evacuated from that area," Smyth continued. "Family members of an extremely high-ranking public official in Ukraine were among them. They were on a train bound for Latvia that derailed in Belarus here, not far from the Russian border, causing mass amounts of casualties. Emergency responders were brought in from all nearby vicinities and the injured were taken to multiple hospitals in both countries."

Cal mumbled a curse as the situation began to become clear.

The LT turned back from the map to face the operators. "Intel indicates the family members in question are alive, but hurt, and were taken to a hospital. In Russia."

A rumble of exclamations ran through the team members in the room.

Smyth continued, "For security purposes, the family was traveling under false names with corresponding fake IDs. Our job is to get the two females to safety before the Kremlin figures out who they've got."

"What about the teams in Germany? They're closer. They can get there faster than we can," Richter, Cal's team leader, commented.

"Since intel suggests the special forces operations in Germany have been closely observed since the invasion of Ukraine, any sudden movement of the crisis-response force from Stuttgart or even

Baumholder could tip off the Russians. The delay in our arrival is a risk, yes, but command feels it's less risky than sending operators from Germany."

Mo held up one hand. "So let me get this straight. While Russia is invading Ukraine, we're going to invade Russia and rescue some Ukrainians?"

"From a Russian hospital," Moose added.

The lieutenant commander tipped his head. "That about covers it."

Mo grinned. "I like it."

Hound Dog shook his head. "You would."

Cal let out a short laugh at his teammates, although he had to admit, there was a certain poetic justice to it all.

The LT continued, "I don't think I need to tell you how critical it is that you get in and out unnoticed. Quick and quiet. International incident wouldn't even come close to describing the clusterfuck that will ensue if a team of US Navy SEALs get caught operating on Russian soil."

Moose snorted. "World War III might come close."

"True that," Slim mumbled.

"When do we leave?" Richter asked, ignoring the running commentary from the team.

Smyth replied, "Wheels up in an hour. Echo team will hold down the fort here while we're gone."

"And the fun never stops," Hound Dog said as he stood along with the rest of the team.

They headed for the cages. There, they grabbed the packs they'd stowed while anticipating they wouldn't be using them again here since they'd be boarding a transport home within the next few days.

He'd checked and packed his gear so many times, Cal worked on autopilot as he grabbed anything he might possibly need including NODs. They'd need the night vision devices in case they patrolled in at night or had to work in the dark in the basement of the hospital.

Their objective might be simple. Get the two women out. But the op was far from easy. And the consequences of failure dire. They trained for urban warfare but this being a fully operating hospital—in Russia—took this op to a whole other level.

CHAPTER TWO

With time of the essence, the hours spent in the air were used for the mission brief. One CIA analyst, two logistics officers and the six-member team plus the Lieutenant Commander crowded around the map showing the area.

Aerial surveillance showed it to be mostly deserted along the Belarus border where the aircraft would drop the team before they patrolled, hopefully unobserved, into Russia.

Dressed as hikers, they'd be picked up by their Russian CIA contact in a van and driven to the hospital where they'd claim one of their friends had been brought after being injured in the train crash.

Working in the team's favor was that most of the really good hospitals in Russia were located in major cities. They'd be infiltrating a smaller facility in one of the villages.

Hopefully, the chaos of the crash would have the overwhelmed personnel distracted enough to not notice when the Russian-speaking CIA operator meeting them at the hospital, dressed in scrubs, led them to the rooms of the packages for extraction.

There was no QRF. If things went south, no quick reaction force was flying in to rescue them. They were on their own.

As the adrenaline pumped hard through Cal's veins, he knew chances of this op going perfectly—of them getting in and out with the two Ukrainian females without incident—looked slim.

That didn't stop them.

As overwatch, Slim and Moose set up a sniper hide outside in the woods in view of the parking lot of the hospital. With them they had two 1980s Soviet-era rifles chambered with Russian rounds instead of their preferred sniper rifles. If either of the two men had to put anyone down, they couldn't do it with distinctly American military weapons or ammo.

The remaining four operators walked through the front door of the Russian hospital, acting as loud and obnoxious as Russians expected Americans to be.

Amid the chaos, Svetlana, their Russian speaking spook clad in scrubs, strolled in unnoticed.

Cal, acting drunk after spilling a liberal amount of beer down the front of him during the transport for believability, caught sight of the elevator doors closing with Svetlana inside.

As Mo pretended he was trying to get the hospital's front desk attendant, who spoke minimal English, to understand his bullshit story about their non-existent injured friend, Cal waited for the communication that would send them into action.

"Third floor. Room 302. Next to the staircase. The packages are together and mobile." Svetlana's voice funneled that good news into all of their ears via their communicators.

Luck was on their side. Maybe, just maybe, they'd get away with this.

Richter tapped Mo on the shoulder and said, for show, "Forget about it. We'll come back to get him when he's released." He turned to face the attendant and asked, in really badly spoken Russian, where the bathroom was.

Looking relieved to be rid of them, the woman pointed to a hallway. There they saw a sign that had visual icons that indicated both the restrooms and, lucky them, the emergency stairs were in that direction.

They strolled leisurely, chatting loudly until they reached the door to the staircase. That is when the drunk American act ended and they snapped into warrior mode.

"Move, move, move," Richter ordered leading the way up the stairs two at a time, the rest of them close at his heels.

They stacked up alongside the door at the third-floor landing. It didn't matter they were dressed in civvies. In action the team still looked like the well-oiled machine that they were.

They trained in close quarters battle but there was nothing like the adrenaline rush of real action. It honed Cal's focus until it was laser sharp.

Like the myopic view in a video game, it seemed as if nothing else existed except the team members and the goal and the obstacles standing between them. No home. No family. No life. No outside world. Nothing but the here and now.

He zeroed in on his team leader in the doorway and the piece of the hallway he could see just beyond.

As Richter said, "Clear," the team moved forward.

They'd each entered the hospital with a pistol in a waist holster at the small of their back. The weapon remained hidden beneath their jackets, accessible but not visible as they tried to maintain the guise of being innocent American hikers for as long as possible.

The fucking room numbers were written in Russian but Svetlana was standing in the doorway to wave them inside.

Richter pulled two flannel shirts out of his backpack and tossed them to the two wide-eyed females to wear. The shirts would make them look like part of the group. The oversized garments would also hide the dirt and blood on their own clothes, which showed the ordeal they'd been through, that they'd changed back into since escaping in hospital gowns was out of the question.

The glaringly white bandage wrapped around the younger one's head was going to be a problem. Cal pulled the baseball hat off his head and moved forward. He adjusted the band to be looser to accommodate the wrapping and gently tugged it onto her head. She looked up at him with a mixture of fear and gratitude and he realized she was probably about his little sister's age.

A closer look at the older woman showed her leg was in a brace beneath her skirt. They'd have to deal with that on the stairs because taking the elevator that opened into the center of the first floor right next to the reception desk was too risky.

They moved as fast as they could, which was still slower going down than it had been coming up.

Richter stayed in the lead as they took the stairs one at a time. Mo and Hound Dog supported the older woman between them, more carrying her than helping her walk. The younger woman followed them and Cal was last, watching their six.

Meanwhile, Svetlana, still dressed as hospital staff, would go down to the lobby via the elevator and meet them outside.

They'd cleared the second-floor landing and were heading for the first floor when Cal heard the door behind him open, followed by a shout, in Russian, that he didn't understand but could interpret well enough from the tone.

The young woman in front of him froze, turning to look at him in fear.

"Go!" he yelled before pulling his pistol from the small of his back. He spun toward the doorway and the uniformed armed guard who'd had the unfortunate timing of stumbling upon them.

World War III.

The words skittered briefly through his mind and he didn't hesitate. Cal pulled the trigger. The suppressor quieted but didn't completely silence the sound of the two rounds. Both hit their mark and the security guard collapsed in a heap.

Cal sprang into action, dragging the body away from the doorway as he looked around him for a place to hide it. He had to buy them time to get away before someone raised the alarm. As the team got farther ahead of him he knew he didn't have even a minute to waste. He dragged the guard's lifeless body down the stairs.

When his team paused at the first-floor exit door, Cal sidled past them. He heard the women gasp at the sight.

Mo raised a brow as Cal pulled the guard past the group but didn't comment.

Cal knew what Mo was thinking but hadn't said. So much for getting in and out unnoticed. But he'd had no choice. The man was drawing his weapon. A shot fired from the guard's unsuppressed weapon, even if it didn't hit Cal—which it very well might have at that close range—would have drawn attention to them. Raised an alarm.

They could *not* be found here. Tensions were too high with countries stacking up on each side of the Russian Ukrainian invasion. Hell, Pelosi's prescheduled visit to Taiwan as one stop of many in the region had already ramped up tension between China and the US to the boiling point. What would a team of SEALs secretly entering Russia to extract two patients and kill a hospital guard do?

World War III.

The rounds in his Glock, 9 mm, was common enough it wouldn't be immediately associated with the American military. He'd grabbed the guard's wallet to make it look like a robbery.

Hound Dog shook his head and said, "Bad timing."

Cal couldn't agree more as he pulled the body beneath the stairs where it wouldn't be found, hopefully, until much later. He did a cursory visual sweep and didn't see any cameras. He didn't see any blood on the stairs either. The two rounds had entered his chest, and the front of the uniform was stained red, but there was no exit wound.

The hiding spot beneath the stairs wasn't perfect but it had to be good enough. There was no time to do better. They might just get out of there if they hurried.

There was a moment where they held their collective breath as they emerged from the relative safety of the stairwell and into the bustling first floor of the hospital. Luckily their presence had already been noted and dismissed from their entrance. The front desk attendant was probably happy when they headed for the front door and continued outside.

They loaded into the van—an old, non-descript piece of shit that looked like a bunch of hikers might use—but they weren't in the clear yet.

Cal breathed a little freer once they crossed the border and loaded onto the bird. But he didn't truly let his guard down until they and the two packages landed at the NATO base in Latvia. And even then, they were still a long way from the camp in Djibouti and even further from home.

CHAPTER THREE

C al woke with a start, jolting from restless slumber to full consciousness like he was back in the war zone rather than stateside and safe.

Although glancing around him at the many displaced and disgruntled passengers crowding Gate A21 of Atlanta's Hartsfield-Jackson International Airport, *war zone* wasn't a bad description.

The gate had become crowded as he'd napped. The travelers were more agitated and contentious than usual as they queued up at the counter. No doubt to make their displeasure known to the beleaguered Delta employee who'd had the bad luck of manning the desk at that particular moment.

When it rained, it poured, figuratively and literally. He glanced out the wall of windows and saw what had been a light rain had, in fact, turned into a sudden deluge of biblical proportions, as rain often did in the South.

Water pelted the windows, bounced off the tarmac, and made it almost impossible to see as far as the plane parked at the next gate over, never mind as far as the runway.

This would probably screw up even more flights. He'd be lucky if he made it back to New York at all at this rate.

Weather had delayed many a flight in his decade long military career and had left him cooling his heels everywhere from Kazakhstan to Rota.

Troop transports were notoriously waylaid. But that wasn't what had happened today.

His commercial flight from San Diego to Atlanta had been delayed for mechanical issues, rather than weather.

Those two lost hours had made his arrival in Atlanta late enough that he'd missed his connection to New York.

With all flights booked full nowadays, the next flight with a seat for him to rebook on wasn't until the morning.

He could rent a car and drive and be there before then, but then he couldn't sleep. And he obviously needed some sleep since he'd just dozed off here amid the chaos.

Standing, he grabbed his bag and moved toward the desk. He wasn't getting on that line, that was for sure. But at six-foot-two he could see over most in the crowd.

He kept his eye on the employee he'd spoken to when he'd arrived, back when there'd been relative peace and quiet at the gate of the flight not due to leave for another two hours or so.

The counter attendant had told him there was still a passenger who had yet to check-in for the upcoming flight.

She was cute and friendly, and he wasn't bad looking himself, so a little flirting and playing the military card had gone a long way. She'd put him on standby for that flight and promised he was first in line for the empty seat in the case of a no-show.

That was before he'd fallen asleep—and before all hell had broken loose.

He glanced at the board behind the desk and saw the word CANCELLED spelled out where the departure time should be.

Well, shit. That explained the panic.

Catching the eye of the woman, he sent her a look that he hoped showed sympathy for her situation.

He hooked a thumb in the direction of the hall that led to the main atrium, where he knew the USO was located. He wasn't going to wait around any longer here at the gate in hopes of getting on a now non-existent flight.

The woman nodded and mouthed, "Sorry."

He shook off her needless apology and gave her a small salute as thanks for her service in this civilian version of combat.

Hiking the strap of his pack higher on his shoulder he spun, only to be waylaid by a wall of passengers who looked like they could easily become an angry mob with a bit of provocation.

Why get mad over things he couldn't control? It was pointless. Besides, he was in no rush to see his old man again. If it wasn't for his concern over his grandmother, he wouldn't care if it took a week to get home.

When the team had gotten back from the Russian op, and then finally to California, he'd turned his cell phone service back on and found a voicemail from home. And another. And then a third. Plus a bunch of emails. All delivered within the few days time he'd been out of contact because of traveling.

One return phone call to his grandmother had him in the CO's office requesting emergency leave.

He couldn't lose his grandmother too. He refused to. Not that there was anything he could do. He was a SEAL, not a doctor.

But he could talk to her doctors. Demand the best treatment money could buy. Make sure they did everything humanly possible.

He knew the importance of advocating for the patient. He'd seen them screw up too many times with his mother. If her cancer had been properly diagnosed earlier…

Then he'd been just a kid. There wasn't anything he could do. He was not a kid anymore and he was making it his mission to make sure his grandmother had everything she needed.

But he had to get home first. One step at a time.

After his short nap, he'd awoken with a man-sized hunger.

Luckily there were plenty of fast-food choices located right there on the concourse. He grabbed himself a quick couple of burgers and wolfed them down at a table in the food court area.

Sufficiently fueled, or at least filled, he made his way down the escalator and back to the main atrium of the domestic terminal.

By the time the sign he sought came into view he'd polished off the rest of the leftover fries he'd carried with him. He pitched the paper bag into the trash and headed for the relative peace and comfort of the USO.

The glass doors of the military welcome center did just that, welcomed him in, as they had countless other active-duty troops and veterans who had passed through this airport, both in uniform and out.

Cal was out of uniform. Since it looked like he'd be spending the night in an airport chair in his clothes, instead of in a real bed in boxers, it was good he could chill in a T-shirt and cargo shorts.

But being in his civvies reminded him he had to get his military ID out of his wallet. He did that before he walked through the doors and up to the desk.

"Hello, there. Welcome." A brunette with the biggest smile he'd seen since arriving in Atlanta greeted him.

"Hello." He slipped his ID card across the desk toward her as she pushed the sign-in book toward him.

"Calvin Swenson."

Pen still in hand, at the sound of her saying his name, he glanced up from where he'd signed. "Yes, ma'am."

Her smile got impossibly wider as she raised her gaze to his. "I was wondering when you'd finally be coming through here."

His mouth opened at the odd comment but he couldn't come up with anything to say, so he got a hold of himself, closed his damn mouth, and grunted, "Mm-hm."

She tipped her head to the side. "What a nice time of year to be in upstate New York."

He frowned. Had he mentioned where he was flying? He didn't think so.

"Uh. Yeah. It should be." His plan was to agree with everything she said as his sole goal became how to get away from this woman.

"I'm Blessing, by the way," she continued.

"Blessing," he nodded, repeating the name to commit it to memory, in case he needed it for a police report or something. He glanced around him. "Just sit anywhere?"

She made a move to come around the desk. "Let me show you to your seat—"

He waved away her offer as another man walked through the doorway. "Please. Don't bother. I'm good to seat myself. You're busy."

"All right. I'm confident you'll find your way to where you need to be. We'll chat again soon anyway," she said, in another strangely prophetic statement.

He nodded and moved away as his head spun. Maybe she knew flights were being delayed and canceled all over the big board and she figured he'd be here for so many more hours they would talk again.

Or maybe she was just an odd bird.

"Oh and Cal."

At the sound of Blessing's voice, he turned back, brow raised.

"Don't worry about your grandmother. Her health is fine."

He opened his mouth again to ask how she'd know that, but he thought better of it.

Instead he nodded and said, "Thanks."

Had he mentioned his grandmother? Yeah, he was a little out of it between all the travel and that nap at the gate but still… he didn't think he'd told her where or why he was flying.

He didn't think more about Blessing or her strange statements as he spotted a sofa and a couple of chairs that looked comfortable enough to spend the night in. Or at least the hours until this place closed for the night and kicked him out—he'd forgotten to ask about closing time. Then he'd have to find someplace quiet to doze until his early morning flight. But for now, he headed in the direction of the seating area.

Nodding to the one guy already sitting there, he dumped his pack on the floor and leaned back against the soft leather, throwing his forearm across his eyes as the length of his journey thus far started to catch up with him.

"Team guy?" the other man said.

Cal lowered his arm. "Excuse me?"

He pointed to Cal's forearm. "Your trident tattoo. East or West Coast?" he asked.

"Coronado," Cal answered, not exactly in the mood for conversation.

"Little Creek," the guy supplied, hooking a thumb toward his own chest.

More receptive to the overture now he knew the guy was in the teams, Cal nodded to the fellow SEAL.

"Nolan O'Rourke. Heading home," Nolan introduced himself while looking like he was not at all happy to be traveling, or maybe just not happy to be traveling home.

Join the club…

"Me too. Calvin Swenson. Heading home to New York," Cal said wondering how many more coincidences to expect.

"Tennessee," Nolan supplied.

Cal acknowledged that with a tip of his head. "Looks like I'm stuck here for the night. My flight was delayed. Missed my connection. No seats until the morning. You?"

"Just a hellishly long layover for me."

Cal let out a sigh. "So here we sit."

"Here we sit," Nolan echoed grumpily.

If he was going to be stranded, it was nice to have a fellow frogman, albeit an unhappy one, to hang with and while away the hours…

That thought was cut short by a new arrival. The soldier who'd entered just as Cal was wrapping up the strange encounter with Blessing.

Dylan Grant, Army, as they learned during Blessing's extended introduction, settled into one of the empty seats in their ever-growing circle. And then there were three…

Shortly thereafter, their number grew to four with the arrival of Chris Andrews, also Navy. Also heading home.

Scott Evers, coincidentally heading back to San Diego where Cal had just come from, filled the last vacant spot in their seating area to complete their circle of five.

And so Cal's long night at the ATL USO began.

At least he had a comfortable seat. And, against all odds, the company turned out to be not so bad either…

CHAPTER FOUR

I t had been years since Cal had been home. Five years to be exact. He hadn't been back for a visit since the funerals, when Pru had wanted nothing more than for him to kiss her and he'd walked away instead.

To her eight-year-old self, newly introduced to the Swenson family when her mom married Guy, Cal had been the sun and the moon. When she was twelve and he'd left for the Navy, he'd been her biggest heartbreak until at eighteen she learned what true loss was after her mom's death.

It was that same year, the year she turned eighteen, that Cal had reminded her of two things—she still had that schoolgirl crush on him and she was still destined to be disappointed by him.

The man she'd dreamed of dating, fantasized about marrying, unfortunately had other plans. Plans that included never calling or texting or hell, even emailing her. For five years.

But it wasn't just her he'd disappointed. Myra got phone calls but not what she really wanted—Cal to come home.

Until now.

"Prudence!"

She put down the coffee cup she'd been about to refill from the urn on the sideboard and turned toward the doorway where she expected the whirlwind that was the Swenson matriarch to emerge at any moment.

"Yes, Myra?" she called as the sound of sensible heels on marble grew closer.

"Didn't you arrange for a car to meet Cal at the airport? I know his flight was delayed and he missed the connection, but he was on standby for another one. I expected him late last night, but I haven't seen him anywhere this morning. His luggage isn't in his room and the bed wasn't slept in. I don't think he's here."

And that was one more thing she was obligated to be grateful to the Swensons for besides room and board and them not kicking her out after she graduated college and should be off on her own—her current job as Myra's live-in personal assistant.

Her *Gal Friday* as the old lady loved to call her. The odd title made Myra happy, so Pru didn't mind it, even if it did make her feel like she was in some old black and white movie.

"I did, yes, and he's not, no."

"Good God, girl. English!" Myra huffed, lowering herself, breathless, into a dining room chair.

While pouring coffee from the ornate silver urn into a porcelain cup for Myra, Pru said, "He's not here yet. The flight he was on standby for yesterday cancelled due to weather. So he's on a flight that will arrive this morning. And yes, I rescheduled the car to meet him."

"How do you know all this and I don't?" Myra asked.

As Pru surreptitiously doctored up the coffee with a spoon of monk fruit instead of sugar since Myra's blood sugar had tested a bit high but she refused to willingly switch to artificial sweetener, she answered, "Because unlike you, I actually check your incoming email."

When Myra told her to arrange transportation for Cal and then email him the details from Myra's account, the twelve-year-old girl's heart inside Pru's twenty-three-year-old body had started fluttering. But even with all the back and forth they'd done regarding the car service and his rescheduled flights, Cal had not said even one personal or friendly word to her.

He was all business. Just like his father. The apple didn't fall far, apparently, even if those two didn't get along.

She pushed that unkind thought aside as she delivered the steaming cup. Setting it down on the tablecloth, she looked closer at Myra, still breathing heavier than looked healthy. "Are you using your inhaler the doctor prescribed?"

"Inhaler. Ha!" Myra let out a very un-Swenson-like snort. "Quacks. All of them."

"I'll take that as a no. He said it would help you breathe better."

"I've been breathing just fine on my own for seventy-two years. I'm not going to get hooked on some drug now."

"You won't get hooked—" Pru stopped herself, knowing it was no use.

Myra's charity group—a bunch of old women with as much excess money as they had free time—had recently taken on the opioid crises as their pet project, so Myra was especially anti-big pharma at the moment.

Not to mention that the breaking news that had hit the anti-drug scene—vending machines that dispensed the life-saving overdose remedy Narcan—had Myra all hyped up. Coincidentally, the Swenson family fortune had been built, almost a century ago, through the manufacture and distribution of *vending machines*.

So the pet project du jour was the drug crisis, the drug companies were the enemy, the Swensons were going to save the world with their life saving vending machines and Pru was going to be hard pressed to convince Myra otherwise. At least until a new cause caught her attention.

But she had to admit that the original Mr. Swenson had been a visionary all those decades ago when he'd bought that old factory in Albany and decided to manufacture vending machines, of all things. Back then, they dispensed peanuts. Three generations later —soon to be four when Cadence finished grad school and got her name on the company masthead as well— Swenson Corp was still the largest distributor of vending machines in the country.

All it took was an idea—well, that and the money to back it. Wasn't that always the way? Money made the world go round. And the people with it got more and more of it. While the people without it...poured coffee for those with it, among other things.

"What time will he arrive?" Myra asked, after a long swallow of her coffee, which she had yet to notice did not contain sugar.

Pru opened her mouth to answer but was interrupted by a deep male voice saying, "If the *he* you're speaking of is me, then he has arrived."

"Cal!" Myra moved to stand, which set Cal into action.

"Don't get up." He dropped his bag on the floor with a thud, and sprinted to her side, hitting his knees next to her chair. "How are you?"

The woman bobbed her gray-haired head to the side. "You know. Good days and bad."

"What do the doctors say, exactly?" he asked, taking her one hand in both of his.

She waved that question away. "I'd much rather talk about you. It's been too long."

He dropped his chin to his chest, giving Pru, who stood behind him, a view of his blonde head and oh so wide shoulders. Not to mention his broad back that narrowed to an impossibly small waist and nice tight ass—

"I know, Grams. That's my fault."

"Yes, it is. But you're here now. How long can you stay?"

"I'm cleared for a month."

A month.

Pru's eyebrows rose at that information. The man who hadn't visited more than a couple of times since he'd enlisted was suddenly home for a month. What the hell?

She couldn't help but wonder what had spurred that decision. His excuse had always been the demands of his military career, even though she knew the strain between father and son was a huge reason Cal stayed away.

None of that had changed, as far as she knew. Yet here Cal was, and here to stay for a whole month.

Her heart gave an involuntary flutter. His being home now brought back visceral memories of the last time he was home. The year she'd turned eighteen. That fateful year when, in her mind at least, her childhood had ended and the trials of adult life began.

In a perfect world, and often in her dreams—both waking and sleeping—Cal would have done so much more than just wrapped her in his arms and comforted her as she sobbed into his shirt. He would have made her his. Made her a woman. Made her forget the trauma.

He hadn't done any of that. He'd been sullen the rest of that very short visit. His encounters with her awkward. His interaction with his father volcanic—

the discord between them smoldered just below the surface waiting to blow.

But that was all in the past. Cal looked good now. And she wasn't eighteen any longer.

A whole month.

A lot could happen in that time. Especially with them both under the same roof. They'd no doubt grow closer. They both loved his grandmother. They both didn't care much for his father. How could they not have a special bond between them just from that?

Of course, he'd have to actually look at her first. Speaking to her would be a plus, as well.

"Cal. Can I get you coffee? Or something to eat?" Pru asked.

As if just noticing the presence of another person in the room, he barely glanced at her as he said, "Coffee would be great. Thanks."

Then he was back to fawning over Myra, cradling both her pale hands in his larger tanned ones like she was made of porcelain.

With a scowl, Pru moved to the sideboard and poured another cup of coffee. Maybe at some point, after she'd served them both, she'd get to that cup for herself.

"Cream or sugar?" she asked, wondering if she'd be

able to capture his attention long enough to get an answer to her question.

In the old days, he took his coffee with both cream and sugar. In the old days, he'd actually acknowledge her presence when she spoke to him, so things had obviously changed. Based on that, she knew better than to make assumptions about anything, even coffee.

"Black," he said, proving her right.

He stood and turned to accept the cup when his barely perceivable pale blonde brows slammed down low over those crystalline blue eyes of his. He cocked his head to one side and said, "Pru?"

"Yes." She laughed. "You didn't recognize me? Have I changed?" She hadn't thought she had. At least not that much. Not enough to have him looking so shocked.

"Uh, yeah. You have."

"Really?" she asked, happy for that if it made him finally notice her. Look at her.

"Of course, you have, dear," Myra chimed in. "You're a young woman now. Not a girl."

"I think it's the hair," he said, still evaluating her.

She'd wanted him to notice her, but this scrutiny as he and his grandmother discussed her and her hair—the bane of her existence—was too much. *Be careful what you wish for.*

"My hair?" More self-conscious than usual, she lifted one hand and ran it over her head.

He nodded. "You used to be all braids and freckles and braces. And now…"

"And now?" she prompted.

"It's good to see you, Pru." He smiled, avoiding the answer she craved.

"You too. It's nice you can stay for a while."

He nodded, his smile disappearing. "I just wish I was home for a more pleasant reason."

She frowned, shaking her head confused. "I don't know—"

"Pru, dear! Can you please get me some fruit from the kitchen? You know what I like. I'm feeling a bit lightheaded. I think my blood sugar is low."

Low? Doubtful since she refused to take the Metformin the doctor had also prescribed. But who was Pru to argue? "Of course, Myra."

Duty called. She glanced at Cal before heading to the kitchen. She'd have to get to the bottom of his strange statement later. This morning was only the first of many conversations she'd have with him while he was home.

Conversations—and hopefully more.

CHAPTER FIVE

"**S**on."

His father addressing him as *son* was a pretty big step up, in Cal's opinion.

Last time he'd been home his father had called him a selfish, ungrateful son of a bitch. That offensive phrase had the word *son* in it, but the intent was very different.

"Dad," he replied, really trying to keep the smart ass, sarcastic tone that had gotten him in so much trouble in the past out of his voice now.

The older man looked perfectly at home pouring himself a drink from the bar cart in the stately bookcase-lined living room. As he should. It was his house…and he never let any of them forget it.

This was one of those formal rooms that he'd run

through but not linger in when he'd been a child. Its wall of French doors opened onto the south porch, which overlooked the sweeping acreage of the estate. That was where he had always preferred to be. Outside in the open air where he could breathe. Where his father rarely ventured.

Cal had grown up here in the house, but the older he got the more uncomfortable he felt. As if he didn't belong. That was probably more to do with this man than the manor. Had his mother been alive, there might be warmth here. As it was, the icy chill from his father reached Cal where he stood across the room in spite of the warmth of the sun streaming through the window.

"Nice to have you home," his father said in a statement that sounded completely devoid of truth but ripe with sarcasm.

"Nice to be home," Cal echoed, equally insincerely. "What's wrong with Grandma?" he asked, getting right down to the point of his visit.

The senior Calvin Swenson, more gray than blonde nowadays, turned, a frown on his aging face. "What are you talking about?"

"She's been to the doctor—"

Cal's father waved a hand. "Oh. That. That's nothing."

Nothing? When she'd told him, she'd made it sound as if her days were numbered. Like if he didn't get home immediately, he'd be in time for her funeral rather than to say goodbye.

Was his father that callous?

The answer to that question was yes. Yes, he was.

Cal flashed back to when he was young and his mother, bald, ailing, but still sweet and beautiful, struggled through chemo. Meanwhile, his father stayed even later than usual at work or in his office at the house *working*.

Calvin Swenson Senior had not shed one tear over the woman who'd born him two children and put up with his bull shit through years of marriage.

Thank God for his paternal grandmother. She had stepped in to raise him and did a much better job than his father and all his hired help could ever have done.

Cal shouldn't be surprised his father had no sympathy. Or empathy. Or compassion. None of what made a person human.

The man was a machine. Built to work, not to feel. Which is why he'd never understand that his son wouldn't follow in his footsteps. Didn't attend his alma mater then go right to the factory, working his way from the ground up, until he took over as the head of Swenson Corp one day.

Cal had been young when 9-11 had happened, only eight or so, but living in New York State, not all that far from Ground Zero in the city, the event had affected him profoundly.

A school mate of his lost a father who worked in the towers. Another, an uncle who'd been a firefighter. Cal's school had provided counseling for all the students.

That event remained the most traumatic of his life until the loss of his mother a few years later. But that September Tuesday was when he'd decided he wanted to join the military as soon as he was old enough. No matter what his father wanted.

"So what brings you home out of the blue? Worried about your inheritance?"

His father's comment might have been meant as a joke—a bad one. Or it might be what he really thought of his only son—which enraged him.

Either way, the statement made Cal want to throttle the man—or leave and not look back. Unfortunately, he couldn't do either at the moment.

"Grandmother called me. I came home because of her." It was the truth and he didn't give a fuck if his father knew it. He definitely wasn't there for his old man.

"At least you show loyalty to one person in this family."

Cal's back teeth were starting to ache from his clenched jaw.

Calvin senior turned, drink in hand, and finally held eye contact with his son. "Well, if you'll excuse me, I have important things to deal with."

His tone made the subtext of that sentence clear. Cal, and his grandmother's health, were not important to him.

"You go ahead, Dad," he said with forced civility as he watched his old man walk out the door before he added, "You sorry fucking piece of shit."

CHAPTER SIX

"Cal?"

At the sound of his name being spoken, Cal turned. Pru stood in the other doorway, glancing around the room, no doubt wondering who he had been speaking to since he was alone in the living room. She hadn't yet realized his father made him crazy enough to talk to himself.

Pushing the unpleasant thoughts of his old man out of his mind, he moved on to a more pleasant subject. Pru and the surprise he'd had finding her here. And finding her so changed.

She looked good. She definitely looked different. All grown up. No longer the gangly preteen she'd been when he'd enlisted. She'd looked older when he'd been back for the funerals, but all he remembered about those couple of days was his own misery and anger at his father and her overwhelming palpable grief.

He lived with the realities of life and death every day. He was trained to deal with death and to take life, but that loss had hit hard. After his mother's cancer, his Uncle Guy's death in the car accident with Pru's mom had been the second biggest blow to rock his family.

As his father's first cousin, Guy wasn't technically Cal's uncle, but Cal had always called him that and loved him as one. More than loving him. Cal had actually really *liked* the man, which was something he couldn't say about his own father. But what he felt about the loss was nothing compared to what it had done to Pru.

But that had been five years ago now. Finding her still living here when he'd been sure she'd have long ago moved out was a pleasant surprise. And a convenient one. From what he could tell, she and his grandmother were close. Which was perfect for his needs.

"Hey, Pru?"

"Yeah?" As she walked farther into the room, looking all too grown up in a dress and sandals, he reminded himself this girl might as well be his little sister.

In fact, Cadence and Pru were the same age. The difference was, Pru was definitely not his sister. Not by blood. Not even by marriage. Which opened up a whole world of things he shouldn't be thinking about her. One of them—the most tame of all his many wayward thoughts—being his wondering if her smooth, deep auburn hair would feel like silk against his skin.

He shook that thought away and asked, "How's Grandma doing? Really."

He wasn't sure what the official deal was, but it seemed as if Pru had stepped into the role of being his grandmother's caretaker. He was grateful his grandmother had a family member for that and not a stranger as hired help for the end of her life.

"She ate breakfast. Now she's reading her newspaper out in the sun. She's old school. I got her a New York Times subscription online and set up an iPad for her to read it on, but she still insists the Sunday Times be delivered."

"How *is* she though? Really," he asked, tired of how the whole family kept sweeping his grandmother's health issues under the carpet like they were nothing. They might have had time to get accustomed to the reality of losing her, but he hadn't yet.

And he was really tired of being in the dark about

the intricacies of his grandmother's health. He was going to have to call her doctor himself. Maybe Pru could get him the name and number...

"She's fine." Pru frowned. "You said something before, about wishing your visit was for a better reason. What did you mean by that?"

"I wish I wasn't home because Grams is sick. Dying." He shook his head, not understanding her confusion.

The furrow in Pru's brow deepened. "What *exactly* did she tell you was wrong with her?"

Now it was Cal's turn to frown. "Why? What's wrong? What are you all hiding from me? As a member of this family, I demand—"

She held up one hand to stop him. "Cal. I'm not hiding anything. I asked because your grandmother isn't sick. I mean not really."

There had to be some mix-up. Maybe Pru didn't even know the truth. Could his grandmother have hid it from her? From his father too? "She called me right after her last doctor's appointment."

Pru nodded. "Yes. Doctor Helman, a cardiology specialist. Last week. I made the appointment for her because she was feeling winded occasionally. They ran all the tests, including a nuclear stress test and determined it's a mild case of COPD. He prescribed an inhaler for her, which she mostly refuses to use, but said she'll be fine. She's also borderline for Type 2 diabetes which could easily be controlled with medicine not to mention a change in diet, both of which she is refusing. But I wouldn't say she's dying or even sick."

Watching him, Pru drew in a breath as an expression of comprehension crossed her face. "What did she tell you?" she asked again.

Lips tight, he drew in a breath through his nose. "Not a lot, but enough to make me believe she was at death's door. I went right to my command and got emergency leave. We're supposed to reserve that for dead and actual dying relations." Not conniving lying grannies.

"I'm sorry, Cal. She's supposed to eat healthy, get some exercise and go in for regular follow-ups with the doctor but, no, she's definitely not dying."

"And you know this for a fact?" he asked, still not believing his loving grandmother, the woman who'd raised him, would lie.

"I was in the room with her and the doctor. I heard it all firsthand."

He stalked to the French doors, biting out a silent curse as he walked. Spinning back, her eyes widened when she saw his face.

"Cal, what she did was bad, no doubt, but I'm sure her intentions were good. I know she misses you," Pru said in defense of the old woman.

He wasn't in the mood to hear it. He was already torn up with guilt that he didn't visit enough. He didn't need Pru reminding him how much his grandmother missed him. But lying—especially about something like this—was unacceptable.

How could he impress upon his grandmother how bad what she'd done was? How it would make him look when he got back to Coronado and his commander asked how his dying grandmother was and he'd have to say, fine.

She needed to be taught a lesson.

Raising his narrowed eyes as he contemplated the best course of action, an idea came to him. He latched on to Pru's gaze and asked, "How would you like to help me get back at her?"

Her already big brown eyes widened further, along with her mouth as it dropped open but all that came out was, "Um."

"Nothing bad. I promise. Just think of it as a practical joke."

She lifted deep red brows. Glancing at the doorway, she took a step closer, putting her at arm's length from Cal.

"You do realize I'm only allowed to live here because of Myra, right?" she asked, her voice low.

Her whisper cut right through him, sending a tingle down his spine as he imagined her mouth pressed against his ear. He shook his head to rid himself of that image.

Shook his head at what she'd said too as he wrestled his brain back to the conversation. Pru should have never been treated like the poor orphaned relation—even if when she was little her red curls did make her look like Little Orphan Annie.

How had her insane mop of hair gone from crazy to crazy sexy anyway? He didn't know how it had gotten to be so sleek, falling smoothly around her shoulders and framing her face like a sensuous curtain, but he liked it.

Before he realized what he was doing, he'd reached out. With two fingers he brushed the piece of hair that had fallen forward off her face.

She stared at him, her warm eyes radiating mingled surprise and confusion and maybe something else underneath. Interest? Desire.

That was a thought for later. Things were complicated enough right now given who she was, who he was, not to mention his scheming grandmother.

He'd ponder what was—what might be—between him and Pru after dealing with his grandmother. And right now, he had to convince her to help him. Or at least not stand in his way.

"Please, hear me out and if you still don't feel comfortable, then I understand if you don't help me."

She drew in a breath and his gaze immediately gravitated to the round tops of her breasts as they lifted and lowered again when she expelled the huff of air. "Okay. I'll listen."

"Good." He smiled.

Revenge on granny and a reason to spend more time with Pru—he probably shouldn't be so gleeful about those two things but he couldn't help himself.

It had been a long time since he'd felt happy in this house. He wasn't going to question it happening now.

CHAPTER SEVEN

"What are you doing outside?" Cal said in a tone worthy of a schoolmarm as his long legs carried him across the manicured lawn and to where his grandmother reclined in a lounge chair with her paper.

Pru watched from a distance, trying to stay out of view. She wasn't on board with his plan, yet she'd somehow been incapable of telling him no.

"I'm reading," Myra replied, putting the paper down as she gazed up at her grandson.

"I don't think you should be out here in the air," he said, reaching down for her arm to help her up.

She tugged her arm back. "Why not? There's nothing healthier than fresh outdoor air."

"If the doctors are that concerned about you, then I'm sure they'd want you to stay in bed. Should you be on oxygen or something?" He made another attempt to lift the older woman.

Again she pulled away. "No. Cal, I'm fine—"

"You told me you were sick," he said, leaving that sentence dangling. Bait, as tempting as a lure on a fishing hook, but Myra was too smart to fall for it.

"I—I am. But the doctor never said I had to be bedridden."

Cal, firmly staying in the role, shook his head. "You need rest and you definitely do not need to be climbing those stairs twice a day."

"For goodness' sake, I can climb the stairs…if I take it slow," she added, not dropping the lie.

Watching the two Swensons going head-to-head was like a master class in stubbornness. Who would win?

That was a toss-up. Pru would have bet on Myra, but after seeing Cal again now, older, more experienced, he could definitely give his grandmother a run for her money.

"Nope. I'm sorry, Grandma. You'll have to stay upstairs. I had Pru call one of those home healthcare agencies. I'm hiring you a full-time nurse. She'll make sure you're comfortable in your room. We'll all come visit you up there. Oh, and I instructed Pru to go through your social calendar. She's sending your regrets for all the events you were planning to attend for the rest of the year."

"What? No! Calvin, you will do no such thing."

"Why not?" He still stood, towering above Myra where she sat in the low lounge chair, but his demeanor had changed.

Gone was the fawning, helpful, sympathetic and devoted grandson. Now, Cal had the look and feel of a predator about him. Waiting. His patience steady and holding as his body was primed and ready. About to pounce as he saw this game—this hunt—nearing its end.

"Why not, Grandmother? Aren't you dying?" he said, pushing her further.

"No. Okay. I'm not." She scowled up at him.

He folded his arms across his chest. "You're not?"

From where she stood, Pru couldn't see his face, but she'd bet he was smiling. One of those Batman villain smiles.

The boy from her youth certainly had changed. Maybe there was more of Calvin Senior in Cal than she wanted to admit. Of course, Myra was no slouch in the take-no-prisoners department either.

"No, I'm fine," Myra admitted, finally bringing her gaze up to Cal's.

"So you lied?" he asked, somehow managing to feign shock.

"Yes. I lied."

"Why?" he asked, sounding sincere for the first time during this sham of a conversation.

"Because I needed you home."

"Why?" he repeated.

"Because I miss you."

"You've missed me for ten years and didn't resort to playing dead. Why now?" he asked.

It was a good question. One Pru was wondering herself.

"There's something going on around here. Something big. Something bad."

Cal drew in a breath, expanding the width of his already broad back. "What's going on?" he asked.

"Prudence, you might as well stop skulking in doorways and come over here too," Myra called out.

Her face grew hot as she walked out of the shadows. "Um, sorry. I didn't want to interrupt."

"Mm-hm. But eavesdropping is all right?" Myra said with a sharp censoring glance like only she could give.

Cal reached out and with a hand on her shoulder, guided Pru to stand next to him. "I asked her to be here."

"Why?" Myra asked.

"Maybe to keep me from throttling you for lying, old woman."

Myra's drawn on brows shot high. "I'd like to see you try."

Cal smiled then laughed. "Feisty as ever. You're definitely not dying. And I'm glad of that. But seriously, Grams. What the hell?"

"Language," Myra warned.

He dropped his hand from Pru's shoulder and she was finally able to think again.

"Screw my *language*. I pulled a lot of strings to get to see you."

She waved that away. "You owed me a visit."

He sighed. "Yes. I know. But I could have put in for regular leave later in the month. I have time saved up. Did I really have to beg command for emergency leave to get here on one day's notice?"

Myra nodded and this time looked as serious as she ever had. "I think so. Yes." She glanced up at Pru, then back to Cal. "We need to talk."

"About what?" Pru asked.

"About the future of the Swensons. Both the family and the corporation."

"Grandma, you're acting like we're in danger."

Raising her pale blue gaze to his, she said, "I fear we are."

CHAPTER EIGHT

"Let's walk," she said as she led them away from the lounge chair she'd just vacated and headed for the garden.

"No. Grandma, you need to sit back down and start talking," Cal warned, taking a harsher tone with her than he ever had.

"Cal. Please. Just walk with me." She turned down the path that led to the fountain and made her way slowly there, stopping to touch a fingertip to a flower now and again as she passed before moving on.

Annoyed, he kept an even pace with her even if the far too leisurely stroll had his blood pressure rising further. This was no time to stop and smell the roses. He wanted answers.

Finally, they reached the fountain. His

grandmother perched on the wide marble lip, the basin broad enough that the spray from the waterspout in the center didn't reach the edge.

"Now. Talk." Cal folded his arms and leveled a glare on her as Pru, who'd been following silently behind, quietly stepped next to him.

"Fine. I just wanted to get somewhere no one could hear us," his grandmother explained.

He frowned at her. "*That* was the reason for this little stroll? Privacy?"

On the seventy-three-acre estate, he wasn't really worried about eavesdroppers. And he certainly wasn't worried about electronic surveillance. On an op, in a foreign city, he might use the sound of the water to cover a conversation. But here? His grandmother had been watching too many spy movies.

"What is this about, old woman?" Cal asked, brows raised.

Now it was his grandmother's turn to raise a brow and deliver a glare in his direction. "I'm not too old to swat your butt."

"You might not be too old to do it, but I'm certainly old enough I'm not going to let you."

"Please. Can we just talk about whatever this threat is?" Pru, the voice of reason, interrupted their bickering, which he had to admit had degenerated to be pointless. Not to mention childish.

"Yes. Please, enlighten us, old wise one," Cal agreed with an eye roll.

"I have this friend…"

Cal let out a huff at that unpromising start.

She shot him a glare then continued, "She warned me. Something bad is coming for our family. Something dark. Something that will threaten Swenson Corp and us personally."

His eyes widened. "That's it? No specifics? Just some morbid fortune teller's prediction?" He'd procured emergency leave and endured a never-ending flight to New York for this?

"You don't understand. I've known Linda for most of my life and she's never been wrong. She knew when I was pregnant with your father even before I did. She knew she'd miscarry every one of the three times she did. And she knew when she'd finally carry to full term and have a healthy baby girl."

"So we're living our lives now based on this woman's track record of lucky guesses regarding babies? Maybe she should work in obstetrics…or on a psychic call line," he mumbled the last part.

"It's not just babies. She…knows things. We roomed together at Vassar. She always knew things before they happened, even back then. I wouldn't believe it if I hadn't personally witnessed so many of her predictions come true. For me and our third suite mate, Agnes. Call Agnes if you don't believe me. She's just an hour and a half away in Mudville. She'll back me up. "

He had no intention of calling Agnes in Mudville or believing any of this bull.

Cal drew in a breath and let it out slowly, searching for patience. "Grandma, predicting what might happen to the people closest to you, people you live with, isn't psychic. It's a combination of intimate knowledge and luck."

His grandmother shook her head vehemently. "No. It's not just us. It's strangers, as well. And it's not just her. Her daughter can do it too. Blessing can look at a person and know immediately things about them."

Cal's gaze snapped to his grandmother. "Blessing?"

"Yes. I know it's an unconventional name, but after the miscarriages, this baby really was a blessing. Goodness, it's hard to believe that was over fifty years ago now."

Jesus Christ. Could it be the same woman? The one from the USO who had seemed to know things Cal had never mentioned. About all of the guys he'd hung out with at the USO. During the hours they'd shared at the Atlanta Airport, it came out that Blessing had said odd, predictive things to all of the guys he'd been sitting with.

She'd told Cal not to worry. That his grandmother would be fine. She'd been right about that.

"Where does this Linda and her daughter Blessing live?" he asked.

"Linda is still in New York about an hour away. Downstate near Poughkeepsie. Blessing was married to a military man. God rest his soul. So she settled down south."

"Georgia?" he guessed, unsure if he wanted to be right or wrong.

His grandmother nodded. "One of the suburbs of Atlanta if I remember correctly."

He drew in a breath, trying to wrap his head around this new information. He wasn't sure if it made him take his grandmother's ramblings more or less seriously.

Either way, he was here now. He might as well stay for the full time of his leave. He did owe his grandmother a visit, even if he was still livid with her. And he wouldn't mind getting to know Pru better— the new grown-up version of her.

Cal expelled a long slow breath. "All right."

"All right, meaning you believe me?" his grandmother asked.

"Meaning I'm willing to hang around here and see if your friend's *prediction* comes true." He held up one hand to stop his grandmother's impending glee which he clearly saw coming. "*But* only until the end of my leave. After that, if anything really does happen, you'll have to call 9-1-1, like a normal person. You know, if any international villainous masterminds come for you or the company."

"You joke now, but it won't be funny when something horrible happens and Linda's predictions come true," his grandmother warned.

With a sigh, Cal glanced down at Pru and saw the look of fear on her face, when he'd expected to see healthy skepticism, if not outright amusement.

"What do you think?" he asked her.

Pru's eyes widened as her focus swung to him. "Me?"

"Yes, you. Do you believe this stuff?" Was this girl so used to being ignored around this house, it threw her off balance when someone asked her opinion. Christ, this family...

She drew in a breath and her eyes cut to Myra before she answered, "I don't know. Maybe."

"What she's not telling you is that Linda had called

me early the morning of the accident. She'd had a premonition involving a car accident and our family. I —I misinterpreted it. Your father was supposed to drive to Manhattan that day for a meeting. I made him take the train instead. He indulged me but that wasn't it. The warning was obviously meant for Pru's mother and Guy. And I missed it."

Glassy eyed, Pru reached out and grabbed his grandmother's hand. "You can't blame yourself for that."

"I know, dear. It's just hindsight and regret are heavy crosses to bear." She drew in a breath then gazed up at Cal again. "Which is why I'm not taking any chances. Do you understand?"

He couldn't believe he was going to say this but the word, "Yes," came out of his mouth anyway.

"So what do we do now?" Pru asked, glancing between them.

"Now I try to investigate a future threat without knowing what it is or where it's coming from. Only knowing it's going to be against our family or the company," Cal said.

"Isn't that what the FBI and CIA do every day?" his grandmother asked him.

He bobbed his head to the side. She wasn't wrong. "Yes, but I'm not FBI or CIA."

"No. You're smarter."

"Gram…" He rolled his eyes at the over the top and baseless compliment.

"And unlike them," she continued, "you have the advantage of knowledge. Of this family. Our history. Our competition. Our enemies."

Did he though? After being away for so long, cutting himself off so completely from everyone except her, did he know anything anymore?

There was that guilt again. Maybe it was time to do something about it.

CHAPTER NINE

"Dad."

His father raised his head where he sat behind the computer screen in his home office. "Cal. How many years has it been since I've seen you in this room?"

Not long enough...

Cal ignored the passive aggressive comment and got right to business. The business of his investigation based on some woo-woo prediction by a possibly crazy lady—believed wholeheartedly by his own whacky grandmother.

"So how's the business going? Company doing okay?" Cal asked, trying to figure out how to find something when there might be nothing to be found, while not knowing what he was looking for.

Not to mention, the hostile witness he was trying to get that information from.

His father's brow rose high. "*Now* you're interested in the business?"

Gritting his teeth, Cal nodded. "Mm-hm."

"Why? You in trouble? Is that why you're home? Are you getting kicked out of the Navy?"

The stream of questions from his father became progressively more insulting. It must have been his anticipation of Cal's failure that had him more interested in his son now than he'd ever been.

"No. I'm not in trouble. In fact, I'm up for a promotion. I came home because Grandma asked me to." No fucking way was Cal going to bring up the Linda-slash-Blessing woo-woo combo. His father would really go off on him then.

"Then why are you asking about the company?"

The better question was, why wasn't his father answering the question? What was he hiding? Was there something here after all?

He had to tread lightly. Act casual. If his father was hiding something, he didn't want the old man to clam up and cover up anything he might have found if he didn't tip his hand.

"Grandma's got it in her head that something is wrong. I promised her I'd look into it. Just to make her happy." Cal waved a hand. A flick of the wrist to dismiss an old woman's ramblings.

"If she's so concerned, why didn't she ask me herself?"

Because you're a mean fuck?

Cal shrugged. "Don't know."

"Well, there's nothing wrong. Everything's fine. You can go back to California happy you relieved the old woman's worries." As his father spoke, he displayed all the cues of someone who was lying.

He wasn't just trained to break bodies. He was also trained to read body language and his father was hiding something. Now this was getting interesting. Oh how he'd love to find what his father was hiding. Then throw it in the man's face.

For now, Cal was satisfied with just saying, "Oh, I'm not going back anytime soon. I'm here for a full month."

He delivered that with a wide grin.

"I'll see you for dinner," Cal said, before turning on his heel and heading out the office door, but not before he saw the stricken expression on his father's face.

This visit might not be so bad after all.

When, in his glee he strode around the corner too fast and walked directly into Pru, almost knocking her down, Cal decided this trip definitely was better than he'd anticipated. And one big reason for that was standing in front of him.

"Ooo. Sorry. Almost took you down." He smiled, momentarily steadying her with a hand on each shoulder. "So what are you up to?" he asked.

"I was just getting Myra a snack. She had a late breakfast but it's too long until dinner so..." She shrugged.

"So you're what? Nurse. Companion. Waitress." He shook his head. If he remembered correctly, this girl had been smart. What was she doing here waiting hand and foot on his grandmother?

"Personal assistant actually," she corrected.

"What kind of business is my grandmother conducting that she needs assistance?" he asked.

"Well, for one thing, I was the one who arranged your car service from the airport and emailed you all those times after the flight changes." There was an edge in her voice when she said it.

It wasn't lost on him. He might not be the sharpest when it came to women, but he knew when one was pissed off. Especially Pru, who always was an open book. And points for him, he even thought he'd figured out why she was pissed.

"That was you emailing?" he asked.

"Yes," she said, just as sharply.

"I didn't realize." That was the damned honest truth. He shook his head, thinking back to those emails. How had he missed they were from her? "Did you sign them with your name?"

"Yes."

He scratched his head. Maybe he didn't scroll down all the way and see her signature. But no. He could swear his grandmother's name was on every one. He shook his head. "I thought I saw Gram's name on them."

"Auto signature," she said simply.

He nodded. Okay. Time to grovel. "Pru. I'm truly sorry. If I'd known they were from you I would have said something. At least a '*hey, how are you doing?*'" He laid a hand on her shoulder and squeezed. "So, how *are* you doing?"

Again she looked uncomfortable to be put on the spot. She shrugged as he dropped his hand from her shoulder. "I'm fine."

"Did you graduate college already?" he asked.

She nodded. "Albany."

He frowned. "I guess I should have known that since Cadence graduated. Where is my sister by the way?"

"You don't know?" she asked, sounding surprised.

He tipped his head to the side. "See? You're not the only one I lost track of. I don't even know where my own sister is."

In his defense, he had gone from a six month-long deployment in Djibouti directly to a flight home thanks to his grandmother's little scheme. There hadn't been much time for catching up on what he'd missed.

"She's in Ithaca." When he frowned, Pru continued, "She's getting her MBA at Cornell."

"Ah." He nodded. "That should make Dad happy. At least one of his children is doing what he wanted."

"I, uh, saw some stuff about Navy SEALs on YouTube."

"Did you now? What did you see?"

"It was a hostage rescue..." she began.

His eyes widened. Jeezus, was his last mission in Russia on frigging YouTube?

"...in Africa back in twenty-twenty."

Phew. He tried to calm himself and nodded. "Oh."

"It's just, what you do is amazing. It doesn't matter what your father thinks."

His lips twitched with a smile. This was her way of giving him a compliment. Supporting him because she knew—she'd have to be completely oblivious not to know—how things stood between him and his father.

"Thanks, Pru. And thanks for being here for Grams. I know you could do or be anything you want —and if that's what you want to do you should go do it. But I do appreciate that you've been so good to my grandmother when I'm not around."

Her cheeks turned the most adorable shade of pink as her gaze dropped away. Finally, she brought it back up to meet his. "I don't mind. I love Myra. But I am glad you're home."

Amazingly, so was he.

CHAPTER TEN

P ru hadn't really slept—as in closed her eyes and woke up eight hours later feeling awake and refreshed—in years. Not since the week she turned eighteen, in fact.

Being a night owl insomniac wasn't as bad as one would think. At least for her it wasn't.

If she'd had to wake, dress and commute to work in the morning, it would suck. But she didn't have to set an alarm to get up or punch a time clock at work. As long as she was available when Myra needed her, she was good.

Those midnight hours, when the house was blissfully quiet and there was no one else around, was found time. *Her* time. Time she could do whatever she wanted. Catch up on a favorite show. Watch a movie.

Read a book.

Sometimes she'd make a cup of tea, sit in the formal living room with one of the leather-bound classics she'd pulled off a shelf in the built-in bookcases, and lose herself for hours.

Sometimes she'd just wander through the rooms, appreciating all the things collected and left behind by Swenson generations past. The large landscape, done in oil by a local Hudson River School artist, Frederic Church, was her favorite. It should probably be in a museum where the public could enjoy it, but she wasn't going to tell the Swensons that.

Mostly, she'd just enjoy the time alone in the house, when, for a few hours, she could pretend it was hers. Imagine she wasn't there as hired help—although, being Myra's assistant placed her firmly in no man's land in that department. She didn't feel quite like family, nor did she fit in with the household staff.

She was somewhere in between. Alone. At least during those found hours, she didn't mind being alone. She loved it.

Turning toward the wall of French doors, she wondered if it was buggy outside. It was a nice night. It would feel good to sit in the garden and look at the stars for a bit—

A noise yanked her from the contemplation of her

plans. It wasn't loud, but she'd definitely heard a sound and it had come from Calvin Senior's study.

Was the old man awake too and working at this hour? That wasn't his usual MO. In all the nights she'd roamed the house after dark she'd never encountered him downstairs after his eleven p.m. bedtime.

So what was it? *Who* was it?

A burglar? The house safe—at least one of them— was in that room but it was kept locked. The only other things a thief might be interested in in there were a few sculptures of moderate value. Maybe some paintings, but there was nothing inside as valuable as the Church in the living room.

Computer equipment… Was that it? Could this be some sort of cyber-attack? Break in, log into Calvin's home computer and get the banking account numbers or something? There was certainly plenty of money to steal—not in physical cash, but electronically— between the family funds and the corporate accounts.

Her body seemed frozen but her mind spun like crazy, jumping from theory to theory as none of them really made sense.

She glanced around her for…something. A weapon of some kind. To what? Disable the intruder with? Or just to protect herself if he turned his attentions to her?

Pru wasn't built for physical combat. She was more yoga and meditation than kick boxing and kicking ass. But she had to do something.

Drawing in a breath, she let it out and made a snap decision. Grabbing the poker from the fireplace, she held it in her right hand and her cell phone in her left, her finger poised over the button to send a 9-1-1 call.

Armed and as ready as she was going to get, she reached for the doorknob—and realized she didn't have a free hand to use to open the door.

Crap. She needed like a holster or something. Shoving the cell down her T-shirt and into her sleeping bra she used her newly freed left hand to grasp the knob. Slowly she turned it until she could ease the door open just a bit.

Heart thundering, she tried to see through the crack and into the room, which was completely dark. Only a sliver of moonlight streaming in through the window lit part of the intricate design of the carpet, which didn't help her at all.

She was going to have to go inside the room. There was probably no one in there, anyway. Old houses creaked and settled, making sudden noises for no reason at all, but she should make sure, just in case.

Pushing the door wider, her right hand starting to

go numb from the tight grip she had on the poker, she took one tentative step forward—

And found herself forced backward against a tall hard body with her neck compressed in the crook of the elbow of one strong arm while a hand covered her mouth.

She couldn't move. She couldn't breathe. And even if she could take in enough air, she wouldn't be able to scream.

The two lamps on the small tables flanking the doorway, which were controlled by a single switch next to the door, flashed on. As soft light replaced darkness she heard a mumbled obscenity as she was released—mostly—and was spun around to face—Cal.

He kept his hand over her mouth as he frowned. "Jeezus, Pru. Shh. Be quiet, okay?" he whispered before taking his hand away.

"What the—"

"Shh," he said again.

Consciously lowering her voice, she said, "What are you doing down here in the dark in the middle of the night?"

He glanced toward the door, moving to silently close and latch it before turning back to her. "I'm finding out what my father's hiding from me."

"What?" It was too late at night and she was still

coming down from the fright of her life. She was in no mood for Cal's riddles—even if his grabbing her was the only physical contact she'd had with him in years.

"I asked him about the company today and I could tell, he wasn't telling me something."

She shook her head, speechless. Given their history, of course Calvin Senior wasn't going to open up and spill everything just because Cal Junior had asked.

Cal held up one hand. "Look. I know what you're thinking. He and I don't talk at all. Why would we talk about business? But I know when someone is lying to me."

"You didn't know Myra was," she pointed out.

With a scowl, he let out a breath in a huff. "Yes. I know. I was blinded by love and loyalty, but I can assure you that is not the case with my father."

"So what do you think you're going to find?" she asked, glancing around the room she usually avoided if she could help it.

Calvin Senior's study was *not* on her nightly tours, for many reasons. Only one of which was her fear he'd catch her snooping and kick her out of the house.

She still wasn't certain he didn't have the room wired with cameras. She wondered about that again as she glanced up at the ceiling, visually scanned the bookcase behind the desk, and even eyed the painting on the wall.

"What are you looking for?" Cal asked.

"Cameras."

He lifted his brows, but he didn't laugh. Instead he drew in a deep breath and let it out with a huff.

"I'd give anything for even a tenth of my equipment back at Coronado. But, for now, I'll have to do things the old-fashioned way," he said as he clicked on the desk lamp and began a systematic sweep of the room.

He ran his fingers beneath the edge of the desk, looked behind paintings, inside and underneath lamps and picked up every knickknack on the shelves.

Finally, he turned to her. "I don't see anything. That's the best I can do for now, until I can get some equipment here."

She was feeling more and more like she was in a spy novel, especially when he sat in his father's chair and pulled open the first drawer.

"Uh, should I stand outside the door and keep watch or something?" She didn't want to.

Getting caught helping Cal would put her position here in jeopardy. But the desire to help him was too strong to deny, fueled by that other desire she'd harbored for him for so long.

He glanced up. "And what are you going to do standing outside the door if you saw someone?"

"Warn you."

"By then it's too late. They've seen you and short of going out the window, I'd be trapped in here. If you were going to keep watch, it would have to be while hiding by the bedrooms."

"Oh. Do you want me to—"

"No. It's fine. The old man drugs himself to sleep every night. He's not coming down."

"How do you know that?" she asked.

"I checked his medicine cabinet before I came down."

He really was good at this stuff. Like James Bond good, but Cal was real and really did this stuff for a living.

"What exactly are you looking for?" she asked as he lifted the calendar blotter on the desk and peered underneath.

"I don't know, but I'll know it when I see it," he said. "Ah, ha. Oh, daddy dear. Didn't anyone ever teach you not to keep your computer password on a sticky note on your desk?"

With an evil grin, Cal woke the computer on the desk, the screen illuminating his face further with an LED glow as he typed in the password.

"Bingo." He announced his triumph as his fingers tapped on the keyboard.

She wanted to stand behind him and see if he was right and there was something to find. But fear kept her from moving from her place of plausible deniability. *"Really, Uncle Calvin. I heard a noise, opened the door and found Cal there."* It wasn't exactly a lie…

Screw it. With reckless abandon she moved farther inside the room until she could see the screen, and on it was Calvin Swenson Senior's email inbox, but only until Cal moved the mouse and hit to change the view to *Sent Mail.*

Smart. She never remembered to empty her sent emails. The deleted emails too. There could be all sorts of things in there to find…even if they didn't know what they were looking for.

"Holy shit," he breathed. He glanced up at her, his eyes wide. "I know what he's hiding."

CHAPTER ELEVEN

Cal's life in the SEALs was challenging—no doubt. Not just the actual missions, but all that went along with the ops. In support of them. Command decisions he might not agree with. Changes to courses of action on the fly. Rules of engagement. Politics. Optics. The media.

But he hadn't realized how many advantages they had. How easily roadblocks could disappear with one phone call to the right person. How information appeared seemingly out of nowhere thanks to countless CIA analysts at work behind the scenes. How he could walk into his cage and get any piece of equipment he needed. And if there was something he didn't have, it would be supplied to him at his request.

Working without any back up now, with no team,

no equipment, no CIA resources, and definitely no cooperation from his father, was a challenge like he'd never faced. Even so, somehow he was going to have to make it work.

He still had his wits, his training, and his experience. And he had Pru. And his grandmother too. He couldn't discount the old woman. She came with a lot of history. Knowledge of the business that spanned decades. And she was the only person his father would back down from.

But were any of them equipped to deal with what he'd found? The answer was no.

The FBI had the resources and the authority to deal with this—if he could trust them in this matter, which he wasn't sure he could.

Then there was the whole family aspect. Exposure could put the family and the company in jeopardy, on multiple fronts. Public opinion. Business contacts. And those less savory and less legal entities Swenson Corp was inadvertently connected to.

Shit. He couldn't believe his fucking father—or maybe he did. It shouldn't be a surprise he should take advantage of the gray areas between what was right and wrong—legally, morally—to turn a bigger profit.

As if this family needed more money. Swenson

Corp's coffers were filled with more money than it would ever need.

And as Pru stared at him with her big wide eyes the color of the rich wood paneling on the walls in his father's office, he was reminded how not all those with the Swenson name had benefited from that wealth.

"What did you find?" she asked, looking almost afraid to hear the answer.

Perhaps she was fearful since their futures were so connected. If Swenson Corp went down and took the family with it, she'd be out of a job and a home.

Although he'd always assumed his grandmother had plenty stashed away for a rainy day. She was raised by a frugal man. Her father, Cal's great-grandfather—began his business during the Great Depression. An experience like that left a lasting impression.

Myra would look out for Pru if anything happened…right? Maybe. Or maybe not. She might believe it would be better for Pru to earn her own way in the world and cut her loose.

The word *practical* didn't even come close to describing his grandmother's no-nonsense approach to life. Particularly in matters of money and business. Which made this whole Linda-slash-Blessing woo-

woo nonsense his grandmother had bought into so strange.

Cal raised his gaze to Pru's. "You don't have to look so worried."

"Sorry, but when a big bad Navy SEAL goes pale and says *holy shit*, I get concerned."

She thought he was a big bad SEAL? The corners of his mouth twitched with delight before he controlled himself.

He cleared his throat and forced his mind off Pru and her pursed lips that she intended to convey annoyance but that only made him want to taste her.

"You should talk about pale. Get outside once in a while," he teased.

"I do. I use sunscreen, as everyone should." She cocked up a red brow and looked even more adorable.

"Anyway… it seems dear old dad is in negotiations with a certain office of the federal government."

"That doesn't sound *holy shit*-worthy."

"It is when he's going to turn over private customer records to the IRS Criminal Investigation Division in exchange for them pulling the strings to give Swenson Corp the exclusive contract for all of the new Narcan vending machines scheduled to roll out across the country."

"Narcan vending machines." Pru's eyes widened.

"Your grandmother is obsessed with that subject. Do you think Myra knows what Senior is doing?"

The door opened. "And what is Senior doing?" Myra asked, hand on the antique knob.

"Her hearing is still sharp as ever," Cal mumbled.

"So is my mind. Sharp as a tack. So talk," Myra demanded. "What's your father up to?"

Cal tipped his chin toward the computer. "Seems he's in bed with the government."

"That's not the only person he's in bed with."

"Grandma!"

"What? As the boss he should know better than to diddle with anyone in the company but there was a certain secretary a few years back... Don't worry. I got rid of her. But I'm waiting for someone to #MeToo that man any day now."

Cal tried to recover from thoughts of his father's sex life, and that his granny had just used #MeToo properly in a sentence and moved back to the subject at hand.

"You know that vending machines are computerized now. Right?" he began, trying to break down the complex scheme into terms she could understand.

"Of course, I know. I'm retired from the company. Not dead. People can pay by credit or debit card. They can also shove in a paper bill and get change. No more needing quarters. So?"

"So, there's also a record of inventory now. An internal memory. Like a counter that keeps track of how many items are sold and how much money was collected. Those numbers have only been stored locally on the machines until now, but Dad is cutting an agreement with the IRS. All new Swenson Corp machines will back that information up to the cloud, which he's granting them access to. And Swenson agrees to service all current machines and retrofit them with the new spy chip."

"Does it actually say *spy chip* in the emails?" Pru asked.

"No. But that's exactly what it is. Especially since I don't think he plans on telling the customers their private info is about to be shared with the government."

The way his grandmother's eyes flared wide let him know she understood the ramifications.

"How much money is Calvin getting in exchange for this?" she asked.

"Not money. Better. Swenson Corp gets the exclusive government contract to supply all of the Narcan machines in the US. Which in the long run will be worth more than any one-time payout."

She shook her head. "I don't care how much the contracts are worth. Doesn't he realize what providing that information to the government will mean? What it'll do?"

"I know. It's crazy." Cal nodded.

Meanwhile, Pru still looked confused. He turned his attention to her.

"Historically, the mob has leaned heavily on vending machines for their *business*," he explained.

"Why?" She frowned.

"It's an all-cash transaction. Or at least it was in the past. Perfect for money laundering. Even with the credit card capable machines, it was still a mostly untraceable income. Until now. Until Dad."

"And his spy chip," Pru added. Cal nodded.

"And I can't imagine they're going to be happy about it," Myra said.

Pru looked from one to the other. "What does this all mean? For us? For them?"

"The authorities never could pin most of what he was responsible for on Al Capone. But they could get him on tax evasion. What my son is doing is a betrayal of the very organization that won't take kindly to that sort of thing. An organization who shows its displeasure in the most permanent of ways." Myra shook her head. "Linda's warning. *This* has to be what she was talking about."

Scrolling through more emails, Cal was going to tell his grandmother he still wasn't ready to take that leap, even if he agreed with his grandmother's assessment of the IRS situation. His father was about to put a big old bull's eye on all their backs. Then one email caught his eye.

It looked different enough as far as subject line and sender that he was compelled to open it. His eyes widened when he did.

"Dad received a threatening email. It says, 'Keep doing what you're doing and you'll be sorry.'" Cal looked up.

"Holy shit," Pru breathed.

"What are you going to do?" his grandmother asked, looking exponentially calmer than Pru, her ever sharp eagle gaze focused on him.

"I'm going to find out who's threatening us and deal with them."

Time to put his SEAL training to good use on the home front.

CHAPTER TWELVE

I n spite of the midnight strategy session held in Calvin Senior's office, Pru was up, dressed and caffeinated before Cal appeared.

He strolled into the dining room, looking better than ever.

How could a man make a blue cotton T-shirt look so damn good? He could be a model for the Gap—if he weren't already occupied saving the world. A superhero in camouflage… and drooling over this man was not going to do her any good.

"Good morning," she said, forcing her gaze and her mind off his bulging muscles.

"Morning. You're up early." He shot her a glance where she sat at the dining room table, a mug and a crumb-strewn plate in front of her. He moved to the sideboard and poured himself a cup of coffee.

"I usually am," she said.

"Why? Grandmother won't be down here for a little while yet... if she has kept to the same schedule she used to have."

She saw the moment he realized he didn't know his family's habits anymore. He'd been away for too long. Ironically Pru, the interloper in the family tree, knew more about the day to day than Cal. "She has. But I like getting up early and having some time to myself."

It wasn't like she would be sleeping if she stayed in bed. Sipping coffee and getting the cinnamon buns hot from the oven beat staring at the ceiling of her bedroom any day.

He nodded and walked over with the coffee mug and nothing else.

"No food?" she observed. "Watching your figure?" She certainly was watching it for him.

A crooked smile tipped up the corner of his mouth. "I was kind of hoping for bacon. Eggs." He shrugged. "Coffee and sweets will just make me jittery."

She couldn't imagine Cal, Mr. Calm, Cool and Collected, jittery. "You can ask the kitchen to make you whatever you want."

He dismissed that with a wave of his hand. "I'm fine."

A frown settled on her forehead. He was so different from the rest. Senior and Myra never thought twice about asking the staff for anything. No matter how difficult. For instance, the Swenson household only used local milk, pasteurized but non-homogenized with the cream still floating on the top, sourced from a nearby dairy. And the bacon Cal wanted but refused to ask for was delivered in bulk to them from a local pig farmer. But when Cadence was home, oat milk and tofu turkey was also kept in stock.

Would all of that privilege go away if word of what Senior was doing with the IRS got out to his customers? If he lost all those contracts because he was exposing critical, possibly prosecutable data, what would happen to the company? Maybe it wouldn't matter if he lost some accounts if he picked up the exclusive contract for every new Narcan machine that would soon be rolled out to every city in the country.

Thinking of last night and all they'd learned from Cal's casual hack job on his father's computer, she asked, "What are we going to do?"

His blonde brows lifted. "It's a nice day. What do you want to do?"

Her eyes flicked wider at the question. In any other

situation she'd love to make plans for a lovely day. Plans that included her and Cal being together. But today was no normal day. "I meant about…" She twisted to glance at the door. "…what we learned. Last night."

His lips twitched again. He lifted his chin toward her cup. "You about finished here?"

She glanced down at the empty mug and plate. "Yes."

"Good." He pushed out of his chair. "Let's go for a walk."

"Where?" She scurried after him, his long legs eating up the distance she had to hurry to cover.

"To the fountain. It really is pretty out there."

It hit her as he held the door open for her and she stepped through and into the morning sunlight, that he didn't want them to be overheard. Or possibly recorded inside the house. And he was right. Even if the mob or whoever else Myra was worried about coming after the Swensons in retaliation for Senior's deal with the feds weren't monitoring them, it would be better if Senior didn't catch wind they knew something. At least right now. There might come a time Cal and Myra would want to confront him. Maybe talk to him about not making the deal.

She realized she didn't know that much about the

structure of the company. Was all the power in Senior's hands? Or did Myra retain some control after the death of her husband, Senior's father?

They reached the fountain and Cal sat on the marble. His cargo shorts displayed his strong tanned calves covered by a fine dusting of blonde hair. Even the man's knees were beautiful. How much perfection could be contained in one human being?

No wonder he'd ran from her bedroom five years ago rather than stick around and kiss her the way she wanted him to. He probably only dated super models in California. Or sexy CIA covert operatives. Yeah, that tracked.

"I need you…"

"What?" Her head whipped up at Cal's words. His snub from five years ago forgotten. The necessity of breathing also forgotten for a moment as her pulse pounded.

"…to do some digging for me."

"Digging?" Did he think Senior had buried something in the garden? She glanced around her at the pristine grounds. The landscape crew that came once a week was not going to like this.

He nodded. "What sort of set up do you have?"

Her brows raised. "What do you mean?" There was probably a shovel in the tool shed.

"Are you running a VPN? How is the house WiFi set up nowadays? Is it just one network connection? And please tell me there's at least a password. Although that won't stop a sophisticated hacker."

Oh. Computer digging. That she could do.

"There's one network for the staff and one for the family. Both are password protected. My computer has a VPN but…"

"You never turn it on?" he suggested.

"No," she admitted.

He nodded. "Well, start turning it on. We need to create a separate private password-protected connection just for you. Nothing else on it. No smart TVs. No Alexa devices. Nothing. Just your computer that's running the VPN anytime it's on. Got it?"

"Yes." Boy, he was kind of bossy when he got in protector mode. She liked it.

"Then I need you to do some research for me."

"What kind of research?"

"You have access to company records?"

"Myra does, and I have access to anything she does."

"Good. To start, see if you can pull a customer list. I wanna see who the biggest clients are. Who would be the most in jeopardy if their records were turned over to the

IRS. There might be a series of shell companies running our machines that are connected but appear separate. I'll have to deal with that later, but first we need that list."

"Okay. I'll get it."

Pru's cell buzzed with an incoming text. It had her jumping, as if the outside world had intruded upon their little spy lair.

She glanced at the display, then up at Cal. "It's from your sister."

"What does she want?"

"Me to tell you to answer your damn texts. That's a quote from her. And also, she's coming home."

His eyes flicked wider. "Now? Why?"

"Why else? Probably to see you."

He scowled.

"What's wrong?" Pru asked. "Don't you want to see her?"

"I'm not saying I put any stock in that Linda woman's predictions, but it would be easier if we didn't increase the number of family members I have to worry about protecting. There's already Myra, Dad —even if he did bring this on himself—and you."

And you.

Cal had included her as part of the family. As someone he was going to protect. Just when she thought she couldn't fall any harder for this man, she felt her heart melt a little bit more.

His hand over hers brought her out of her own thoughts. "You all right?" he asked.

"Yeah. Never better." She shot him a tentative smile.

The mob might be after them. Even if they weren't, if Cal Senior caught her downloading company information, he'd kick her out and she'd be homeless. But Cal was here, with her, watching out for her, and somehow that was all that seemed to matter.

That, and his hand on hers.

CHAPTER THIRTEEN

C al tugged at the tie around his neck. It felt like a noose.

He'd rather patrol twenty miles in full kit than wear a suit and tie for the next eight hours but he had no choice. In the world he was about to infiltrate, this was the armor he needed.

His dad didn't know it yet, but Cal had declared that today was bring your adult son to work day at Swenson Corp. For lack of any other place to look for threats until Pru got him that customer list, he decided shadowing his father was the best immediate course of action.

He had to blend in, not stand out. Look the part of the Swenson heir apparent preparing to take his place.

Hence the suit.

He stood in the dining room, standing rather than sitting to sip his coffee. Leaning slightly forward as he was careful to not dribble on his clean shirt.

That's how Pru found him when she walked in and came to an immediate halt. "You're really going to the factory?"

He scowled. "You wouldn't catch me in this if I weren't."

Her lips twitched with a smile. "I think you look nice."

"You don't have to be choked by this tie all day," he grumbled.

Her smile bloomed, widening until it reached all the way to her eyes. "Try wearing high heels sometime."

"Yeah, no thanks." He let out a huff and put the coffee down. It was too stressful to drink black coffee while wearing a white shirt. He'd stick with water for the rest of the day.

"I have something that might cheer you up."

At that, he glanced at Pru and saw a file folder in her hand. "Is that…"

She nodded. "What you asked for."

His gaze shot from one entrance to the room, to the other.

"He's gone already," Pru answered his unspoken question.

"Already?" Cal had thought he'd gotten up early enough that he'd beat his father downstairs, which is why he had yet to see the man today. Apparently not.

"He leaves super early. I think he likes to catch his employees trying to sneak in late."

"That tracks." Cal nodded.

Pru moved closer and he got a whiff of something fresh and clean. He leaned forward as much to take the folder as to smell her.

What was that? Her shampoo maybe? It was too light and fleeting to be perfume. He liked it.

He also liked the stack of papers inside the folder. Although he was going to have to sit to really study them.

"Let me give you a summary. At least as far as I can tell from looking at the list of customers, for both purchases as well as service contracts going back as far as we have computerized records. There are the big corporations, of course. Retail giants like Walmart. The big hotel chains that have vending machines on every other floor. There are municipalities putting them in public buildings, like courthouses. That all seemed perfectly normal. But it was the clusters of individual businesses that have machines, close groupings but separate owners, that stuck out to me."

He lifted a shoulder. "I suppose that will happen in the larger cities."

She moved to stand behind where he sat with the list in front of him. "Yes. It could. But I googled the exact locations. Some are near but not in major cities. And what's strange is that so many of the machines are in mom-and-pop shops in residential family neighborhoods. Not in the bigger commercialized areas."

"Did you keep note of where some of these clusters were?" he asked.

She nodded and reached down to flip to the back of the folder where she'd left a sticky note.

He read from the list. Brooklyn, Queens, Manhattan, Staten Island. Long Island. Philadelphia. Pittsburgh. Buffalo. Providence. Hartford. Boston.

Cal didn't deal with the mafia as a SEAL. He knew far more about Boko Haram than he did about the Bonanno crime family. But he knew enough and these cities were known mob hot spots.

He glanced down at the last two names on Pru's list. The final one she'd underlined and marked with two exclamation points.

Albany. And Apalachin, which if he recalled

correctly was a small town about two, two and a half hours away.

When he glanced up at her, she said, "So I googled *mafia in Albany, New York...*"

God help him. He'd gone from having countless analysts from a dozen different departments at his disposal, to this. Pru and Google.

"There's a whole article, Cal. The FBI set up an office in Albany just for the mob. Well, there was also some communist scare involving General Electric and airplane parts." She dismissed the detail with the flick of a wrist. "But a big part of their focus was cracking down on mobsters."

He flipped back to her list. She'd alphabetized it by location. That was how she'd spotted the clusters. Smart. He'd been more focused on looking at the entities who owned the vending machines. And if she was right, and these clusters were mob owned, and damn close to the Swenson factory and home too, he needed to look into this.

"What are you going to do?" she asked, looking as concerned as she was excited.

"It looks like I'm taking a little drive." He could check out all the addresses in Albany, and there were a lot of them, but as the state capital, as well as a college town, a lot of those could be legit. But the cluster in Apalachin—*that* one he wanted to see for himself.

He hadn't planned on a road trip today but the information warranted action. And if SEALs were good at anything it was pivoting.

The good news? He could take off the fucking suit and tie. It was worth driving to Apalachin just for that reason.

"What should I do?" Pru asked.

He'd expected nothing but a printout from her and he'd gotten an insightful analysis instead. Time to give her something more challenging. He'd bet she'd rise to the occasion beautifully.

"How do you feel about doing a deep dive into the Narcan industry? What companies produce it and where? The product cost. Any regulations regarding distribution. That kind of thing."

Her eyes widened momentarily before she slowly nodded. "Okay."

"I want more details on the product and the industry my father was willing to sell his soul to the IRS to get the exclusive vending contract on."

Pru nodded. "I'm on it."

"Thanks." He tugged on his tie one more time, loosening the knot. "I'm gonna change and get going."

She watched him stand, her gaze tracking him as he moved toward the door before she said, "Cal?"

"Yeah?" He paused.

"Be careful."

He'd survived a lot in the teams and he planned to survive much more over the next ten years or so before he retired. And if his number came up during one of those ops, he'd die happy, knowing he did so doing what he loved and in defense of his country.

But there was no way in hell he was dying in damn Apalachin, New York.

"No worries." He shot her a smile then reached up to completely pull off the tie. He'd take body armor over business attire every damn day of the week.

CHAPTER FOURTEEN

"Surprise!"

Cal had only been gone for maybe ten minutes when Cadence walked into the dining room and announced her return.

Pru's eyes widened. "Cadie. Hi. You didn't say you'd be home today." She stood and moved to hug her friend.

"That's the whole idea of a surprise, silly." Cadence smiled, flashing brilliantly white teeth before turning her sky-blue eyes that looked so much like Cal's toward the sideboard, "Coffee. Thank God. I don't suppose there's oat milk?"

"Not out here. But if you ask in the kitchen—"

Cadence waved away Pru's suggestion and turned

with a cup in her hand. "How have you been?" she asked with an exuberance that only she possessed.

"I'm good."

But obviously not as good as Cadence who was, as usual, sheer perfection.

Cadence's long blonde hair was precisely cut and parted down the center to frame her face like an ephemeral curtain of gold. If Pru had to guess, Cadence had had it professionally washed and styled that morning, judging by the smooth shine and effortless looking soft waves that she knew were anything but. It bounced and swung against her back as she moved, but in spite of her hair looking flawless, Cadence had tied a bandana around the crown of her head, giving her a stylish boho look.

And the clothes… Pru wouldn't say she was jealous. Or envious even. What she felt was more awe. Like what one felt at a museum while looking at a priceless work of art. It was beautiful to look at, but it wouldn't fit into her own life.

Owning, and actually wearing, the clothes that Cadence did—and did so well—would be like Pru having a Picasso hanging on the wall of her attic bedroom. Ridiculous.

Pru couldn't carry a Chanel purse on a daily basis

like Cadence did. She'd spend the whole time worried she'd scratch or stain it.

But for Cadence, there was no doubt, she pulled her high-end style off perfectly. Something Pru had accepted years ago.

Pru tucked a piece of her own hair behind her ear and tried to ignore that the sole was starting to pull away from the body of her favorite pair of Converse. She'd bought them secondhand for nine bucks at Great Finds, her favorite resale shop in Albany, where ninety percent of her clothes came from.

At least, that's where she used to shop when she was commuting to college for four years.

Gosh. She hadn't been there in a long time. She missed having that time to herself to slip away to that little shop and hunt for a great find at an incredible price.

Shopping in Great Finds was like searching for gold, and actually finding it. A lot of work but worth it every time she'd walked through the door. And the profits when to charity. What was there to not like about that?

Cadence, on the other hand, was wearing a skin-bearing Free People scarf-style halter top, platform shoes and black Lululemon high rise, flared leg bottoms that—if Pru weren't mistaken—would have cost Cadence well over a hundred dollars off the rack at the store. And there was no doubt in her mind Cadence had bought everything she had on new.

She also wasn't going to tell Cadence she'd seen Lululemon pants at the thrift store for ten bucks. Along with Hollister, American Eagle, and Urban Outfitters at a fraction of what they cost new. Admittedly, a couple of those discoveries were currently hanging in Pru's closet.

That was the one good thing about her little attic bedroom. It came with a killer closet. The ceiling was low and slanted but it was technically a walk-in and she loved it. And she loved the look of how she'd hung her clothes, organized by color, on dozens of all new pretty pastel pink matching velvet hangers she'd splurged on at the dollar store.

Of course, Cadence's closet was as big as Pru's whole bedroom. But as put together on the outside as Cadence was, her closet was a disaster on the inside. Messy. Unorganized. Packed so full things were impossible to find.

Pru wouldn't trade closets—or the clothes inside— with her friend for anything. She would however love to have the wall of built-in bookcases with the window seat in Cadence's room. She'd fill it with all her treasured thrift store book finds.

It seemed like almost every room in this big old house had a bookcase…except hers. Maybe one day she'd splurge and order one…

"So what are you up to nowadays?" Cadence asked, pinching off a piece of the croissant on the plate she'd laid on the table when she'd sat.

"I'm still working for Myra."

"I mean what do you do for *fun*," Cadence emphasized.

Fun? What was that?

Pru avoided saying that she was having fun doing the research projects Cal asked her for help with but she didn't think that would go over well with a party girl like Cadence. So instead, she just shrugged and admitted, "Not much."

"Well that's going to change. And right now too. I'm home and we're going out."

"Out? It's like ten in the morning."

"It's never too early for fun," Cadence said, perfectly seriously.

The phrase should probably be on a bumper sticker on Cadence's car. *If* Senior would allow bumper stickers on the new white Tesla Model S he'd gifted his daughter to celebrate her starting at Cornell.

At least the car was electric and good for the environment even if it was outrageously expensive.

The sound of tiny doggy nails against the hall floor had Pru glancing toward the doorway just as Peanut came running into the room. At least running as fast as a dog so small it fit in a large purse could run. Cadence's Louis Vuitton purse, to be exact.

"Hello, Peanut," Pru said, leaning down to rub the dog's face after the tiny ball of energy ran over to her and paused his perpetual motion for a few seconds. "Where have you been until now?" she asked in a sing-song voice appropriate for both children and pets.

"I had the gardener take him for a walk so he could pee and poop after the car ride. Then I *hope* the kitchen staff gave him some water and a treat like I asked them to," Cadence answered as she bent and scooped up the miniature French Bulldog that had run to her.

Even Cadence's dog looked fashionable in a tiny, studded collar that was probably also designer.

"So, back to our girl's day out. I'm thinking we'll hit the salon for makeovers and then a shopping spree. My treat."

Pru cringed. She hated when Cadence wanted to do expensive things and then offered to pay because she knew Pru couldn't afford it. "I'll have to make sure Myra doesn't need me here today."

"You let me handle Grandmother. Go get changed. Then we'll leave."

Pru glanced down at her outfit. She hadn't been planning on changing but... what Cadence wanted, she usually got. "Okay. I'll be down in a few."

As soon as she put together an outfit that looked half as great as Cadence's. Her best friend could be a lot of work sometimes. But she loved her anyway.

It was more than a couple of minutes, but finally, Pru had put together something that wouldn't make her embarrassed to stand next to Cadence in public. She had on faded jeans with the perfect number of holes in them, and an off-white tank top with a matching lightweight but slightly oversized cardigan, worn open—she wasn't as comfortable showing as much skin as Cadence was. On her feet she had camel colored leather sandals with a chunky heel.

Trotting down the back stairs from her bedroom, she got to the main hall just in time to see Cadence making her way down the grand staircase.

"Grams said it's fine. You should take as long as you want today and said to have a good time. And she even gave me money to treat us to lunch."

Things always did go more smoothly around there when Cadence was home.

"That's nice. Thank you for asking her." Relieved

her friend was in the same clothes and hadn't changed into an even more fabulous outfit, Pru was starting to look forward to the day.

"You look nice," Cadence said when she reached the bottom of the staircase.

Pru scowled. "Okay, what's wrong with my outfit? What should I change?"

"Nothing. I said you look cute."

"You weren't being sarcastic?"

"No, but now I think I was just insulted."

"No. You weren't. If anything I was insulting myself. I know I don't have your fashion sense. I just assumed I'd done something wrong."

"Well, stop assuming. You totally nailed the Coastal Grandmother aesthetic."

Pru widened her eyes. "The what?"

"Coastal Grandmother. It's casual. Comfortable. Like what you'd wear in a beach town at night to go out to dinner if you were like a middle aged, divorced woman. Pretty much exactly what you have on now," Cadence explained.

Looking like a middle-aged divorced woman was a good thing? Pru would never understand fashion. But she did like the casual and comfortable part and Cadence approved so she'd go with it.

"The name was coined on TikTok by a twenty-six-year-old in California who went viral. It was all over BuzzFeed. Do you not read?" Cadence accused.

Pru did read, but books. Not BuzzFeed.

"Sorry. Must have missed that. But okay. Since I'm in style, I guess I'm ready to go." Pru swung her purse onto her shoulder.

Cadence's gaze snapped to the weathered brown leather saddlebag. "Is that my grandmother's old bag?"

Darn it. She'd been caught digging through Myra's hand-me-downs.

"Um. Yes. But it's Coach and she was going to donate it. So I grabbed it out of the bag before I dropped off the donations."

Cadence cocked up one blonde brow. "Nope. Nuh-uh. That purse looks like it belongs to an old lady because it did. If you want a Coach, get this season's cute little baguette bag."

Pru frowned and considered the boxy bag with the brass buckle hardware at her side. "I thought it was classic. And I thought looking like a grandmother was good. Coastal Grandmother. Remember?"

Cadence's expression told Pru what her friend thought of her opinion.

"No." Cadence shook her head. "Come on. We're getting you a new bag today too."

"I don't need—"

"I won't hear no for an answer. I told you, my treat."

Her friend buying her a pricy purse was what Pru really didn't want. "Cadence, I'm not going to let you—"

"Stop. I didn't have a chance to get you anything for your birthday this year so you have to let me make up for it now. Besides I have to stop by one of the department stores in Albany anyway to grab something at the makeup counter, and they sell Coach, so no arguments."

Pru drew in a breath and sighed. "Okay."

Cadence was a force of nature. Like a storm at sea. A smart person knew when to not fight it and just ride it out. And since she was already dressed like a grandmother at the beach, she might as well hunker down and ride out the storm.

It looked like she was getting a new purse. And darn it, she was starting to get excited about that, in spite of herself.

CHAPTER FIFTEEN

Apalachin, New York. Population approximately eleven hundred according to the census and Pru's research, a folder of which Cal had riding shotgun on this road trip.

There was a diner, an ice cream stand and a restaurant that belonged to one of the smaller chains. A walk-in healthcare facility located in a strip mall with a bagel shop and a design studio. But amid all the random commercial ventures scattered among what seemed like perfectly normal residential neighborhoods were over four dozen vending machines, according to the Swenson Corp's customer records. That was about one vending machine for every twenty-three residents.

That was the same ratio for the country of Japan,

which had the highest density of vending machines per capita in the world. But this was Apalachin. A town that did not attract tourists or crowds in any way. Even with close to seventy percent of all vending machines being owned by small businesses, the cluster in this tiny town was a red flag.

Cal *might* have wondered about the high number, *if* this wasn't Apalachin, a town well known for its mob connection.

Any routine Google search would reveal the town's mob history. It was no secret. But it was interesting. Were they bold enough to keep operating in a town where they'd already been caught? Or were these machines remnants of a past time? Part of the landscape now, forgotten. Legit enterprises and not for laundering money.

That's what he was here to find out. Although how exactly to go about it he wasn't sure. Getting a feel for the place was a good start. A keen power of observation was important. It had saved his life more than once.

He parked his 1996 Ford Bronco on the main street and got out. He smiled as he patted the hood. He'd loved the used vehicle since the day he first laid eyes on it with the *For Sale* sign in the window.

It was the first vehicle he bought for himself. It had

been old as hell already when he'd turned sixteen and got his license. His father told him it was a piece of shit, which made him want it even more. So he'd used his own money.

He'd only used it for a few years before joining the Navy, but even so, he hadn't realized how much he'd missed it until driving it again now.

Miraculously—the inspection and registrations had been kept up to date. It had even started right up, as if someone had been caring for it in his absence. He supposed he had Pru to thank for that. His father wouldn't give a crap but his grandmother might. And she would no doubt delegate the duty to her unlikely assistant.

Pru was a subject he'd have to ponder at another time. He had a location to scope out.

He pocketed the key ring that still sported his old house keys, and the key he'd duplicated for the gun closet. He'd had the key made after his father wouldn't let him use his grandfather's gun right after he passed, even though Cal had been shooting the weapon— under his grandfather's tutelage—since he'd been a kid.

He consciously relaxed the tension in his jaw that thoughts of his father caused and glanced around. Right in front of him was a hair salon. That was always a place for lots of chatting by the locals. He opened the door and sent the bell above his head tinkling.

"Hello." An older dark-haired woman with bright red lips sent him a smile, while the few others in the room looked him up and down, assessing the stranger in their domain.

"Hi. I was wondering if I could get a haircut."

His hair was on the long side, as with most SEALs. They didn't need to keep it short, the special nature of their service making them exempt from that particular Navy rule. And even though with his light coloring there was no way he was blending in, say, in a Muslim country and didn't need to have the long hair and beard for cover, he'd gotten in the habit of letting his hair get shaggy.

He had a month to let it grow back in. By the time he was back in California, he'd match the team as well as the surfers.

"Sorry, sweetie. I'd love to get my hands in that angelic hair of yours. But ladies only here at Rosanne's. But you can hit up Rocky's. It's the barber shop just up the road a couple of miles."

He'd have to shift gears. Head for the diner, sit at the counter and order a nice big meal that would take him a long time to eat—and listen. Then head over to

Rocky's where he'd bet he'd find a vending machine or two, just like Rosanne's had.

"Okay. Thanks." Cal nodded and was about to turn for the door when he heard an excited squeal followed by some loud voices. All female. He turned back to the woman with interest. "Party going on back there?"

She shot him another smile. "Something like that. Have a great day. Tell Rocky that Rosanne sent you. He'll treat you right."

"All right. Thank you."

Damn. He'd been very politely but firmly dismissed. This place held so much promise for his recon. He could only hope that Rocky's would too.

One club sandwich with a cup of chicken soup and a couple of miles drive later and though the diner hadn't yielded much in the way of intel, Rocky's Barber Shop did not disappoint. It was like stepping into a mob movie.

He could have been in a barber shop in Brooklyn or Chicago where the *connected* men of the town sat around for hours and not because they were waiting for a haircut. More social club than barber shop, this was the town's hub for news and Cal was ready to soak it all in.

This time when he asked if he could get a haircut, the answer was the sweep of a hand to indicate the empty chair and the crisp flip of a barber's cape that was secured around his neck.

Cal eyed the straight edged razor on the counter just as Rocky, whose shoe polish black dyed hair spoke to his vanity, sent the back of the chair backward putting Cal in a position he didn't love as Rocky insisted he give Cal a shave first.

He forced himself to relax. There was no reason for him to feel threatened aside from habit. He was home. He was safe. It was just a damn shave and a haircut, for God's sake.

"So, how's your old man doing?" Rocky asked, sending Cal's eyes wide.

"Excuse me?"

Razor in his hand, Rocky turned back to Cal. "You're Swenson's son, am I right?"

Oh, shit.

"Uh…"

"Ha-ha. Look at his face!" One of the men seated in a row of chairs along the front windows laughed and pointed at Cal. His voice—heavy with the telltale accent of Brooklyn—gave him away as being a transplant to the area.

Rocky shot him a glare. "Cool it, Vito. Stop harassing my customers or you can get out."

Vito scowled as a silver-haired man seated next to

him, whose well-fitting suit emitted a different vibe than Rocky—a quiet elegance or maybe just wealth and power—stood and wandered closer.

Cal's SEAL training kicked in. He assessed the situation and his options as the man approached. Meanwhile, Rocky still towered above Cal in his prone position, reclined in the barber's chair. The man reached for a covered slow-cooker and pulled out a small white steaming towel and Cal wondered if he was about to be smothered with it or enjoy the best shave of his life.

He needed to buy time and see which way this situation went as he keenly felt his lack of a weapon. Any weapon. Even his great grandfather's .22 revolver or at least a hunting knife. He gauged the distance to the straight razor as he said, "I am, actually. Calvin Swenson Junior. Although I go by Cal. Keeps the confusion to a minimum."

The gray-haired man stopped next to him and extended one hand that sported a large gold ring. "Vincent. I knew your grandfather."

That was a twist he hadn't been expecting.

"Did you?" Cal said while shaking the man's hand. He had a firm grip. Firm but not threatening. Just confident. Like a man who didn't need to prove to anyone that he was powerful.

Vincent tipped his head. "I sent an arrangement to the funeral when he passed. Please give my condolences to your grandmother."

"Thank you. I will." Cal tried to not let his confusion over the turn of this conversation show.

He would like to believe this conversation meant he wasn't about to have to defend his life against three old men with a straight edge, but he knew better. The mob was nothing if not polite. He wouldn't be at all surprised if these pleasantries were followed by an apology and then his attempted murder.

Attempted because Cal could probably take all three out. He was young and fit—in the best shape of his life physically. Situationally aware and prepared for an attack. And extremely well-trained. They—he'd wager —were not any of those things.

Rocky stepped behind him with the hot towel and draped it over his face. His whole face, blocking his sight and leaving only his nose exposed so he could breathe. Shit. He did not want to be in this position, but he also didn't want to spur these men into action if it could be avoided.

"What brings you to our little town?" Rocky asked.

Lie? Or tell the truth?

As Rocky unwrapped the towel from his face, Cal

made a split-second decision. "I suppose I'm here looking for answers."

Rocky let out a laugh. "Not many people come to Apalachin looking for that."

"Yeah. We're more in the secret keeping business, if you know what I mean," Vito spouted, earning him a raised eyebrow from Vincent.

"What are you looking for, son?" Vincent asked.

Cal was as much taken aback by the term—son—as the gentle warmth with which it was delivered.

"It's going to sound crazy." In fact, he was starting to think he was a bit mad employing this Hail Mary of honesty.

The three men didn't respond to that comment. Because they knew silence was the best way to keep someone talking? Or because they had nothing to say? It didn't matter.

Cal continued, "My grandmother got a strange call from a friend of hers—" He couldn't believe he was actually saying this. And to these men of all people. "It was a warning of sorts from an old college friend of hers."

"Linda." Vincent's mention of the name had Cal's head whipping up.

"Yes. You know her?"

Vincent nodded. "Not personally. But I know of

her. Your grandfather used to talk about her. And her predictions. Used to drive him crazy how seriously Myra took them. Until they started to prove true."

Cal's brows shot high as he tried to wrap his head around all this information.

"What did she predict this time? And what's it got to do with us? Here?" Vincent asked as Rocky and Vito stood by silently.

"Maybe nothing. This part—Apalachin—was all me. All Linda said was that the family and the corporation was in danger. So, to humor my grandmother I started digging."

"Digging usually turns up things you don't want to find," Rocky mumbled and Vito nodded.

Cal wasn't going to lie to himself. Part of him wanted to out his father's behavior to these men before his self-serving deal with the IRS could harm them. These strangers had treated him with more respect than his father had shown him since his return. But there was another part that knew cold hard honesty could protect his family and the company.

Linda's odd warning aside—and he wasn't ready to credit her or her daughter Blessing with any powers of prediction just yet no matter what Vincent or his grandfather had thought— Cal knew that what his father was doing was dangerous. Threatening the business enterprises of men like these was not smart. But if it was all out in the open, it could prevent the mob from acting. They didn't know if his family was or was not under the protection of the FBI.

He cut his gaze to Rocky. "That's exactly what happened. It seemed I found out something about my father's business dealings at Swenson Corp that concerned me. Something that could affect your enterprises."

"And you're here to warn us?" Vincent asked, looking doubtful.

"More to see if there's anything I or you need to be concerned about."

"Quit dancing around and spill it," Vito interjected.

One more look from Vincent had the man backing down.

"Swenson's new vending machines, and any of the old ones that are under service contracts, are not only going to be outfitted with inventory and income tracking capabilities, but that information will be able to be turned over to the IRS." Cal didn't have to spell out what that would mean to any money being laundered through those machines.

He expected them to be concerned. Angry even.

What he didn't expect was all three to break out into raucous, knee slapping laughter.

"You think we don't know that?" Rocky asked, shaking his head when he finally caught his breath.

"Pretty boy here thinks we're stupid," Vito accused.

"Son," Vincent said with a smile. "We've assumed every transaction was being monitored since the first machine capable of taking debit cards rolled off the Swenson assembly line. The only surprise is that it's taken this long for the feds to figure that out."

Cal frowned.

"You look confused," Vincent observed.

"I guess I am. Why do you still have so many machines in this one little town?" He left the end of his thought unspoken… *If they could no longer use them to hide illegal money?*

Vincent lifted one shoulder. "They earn good money. And people in town seem to like them."

Rocky nodded. "Yeah. My two out front really raked in the dough during Covid when no one wanted to go into a store for a soda or a candy bar. Couldn't keep the damn things filled."

"What are we supposed to do if we did want to get rid of them?" Vito scowled. "Take pennies on the dollar selling them used? Fuck that shit. Why not let them keep earning a little dough?"

Cal blew out a breath, surprised, but incredibly relieved.

"That ease your worry any?" Vincent asked.

"Yes," Cal admitted.

"You ready for that shave and a haircut now?" Rocky asked.

Why not?

"Sure. Thanks." He relaxed back into the chair.

Vincent leaned back against the counter eying Cal. "So, how is Myra? Still as pretty as ever?"

Cal's brows shot up as Rocky approached him with the straight edge. But for the first time since arriving, he didn't wonder if he was about to get his throat cut.

He did, however, wonder what had gone on between his grandmother and the man who was apparently the head of the Apalachin branch of the mob.

CHAPTER SIXTEEN

After Cal drove off that morning, Pru had all intentions of getting right to the project he'd assigned her... after she'd settled Myra into some activity or another to keep her busy. But of course that plan had been waylaid not only by Cadence's sudden appearance but their girl's day out.

There was the impromptu makeover. And shopping spree. And lunch.

Cadence had always liked to be Pru's fairy godmother. And when Pru could conquer the uncomfortable feeling and weirdness of Cadence paying for everything for her, she did try to enjoy it. Mostly she treasured the time together again with her friend who'd been away more than she'd been home since boarding school.

CAT JOHNSON

She had to admit being pampered for hours, having her nails and toes done and her hair trimmed, conditioned and highlighted, was a treat. But it also meant that when Cal returned today she would have to tell him she'd done nothing to research Narcan.

Maybe he'd be late. It was a pretty long drive to Apalachin, there and back. And that didn't account for whatever time he spent in town, looking around.

Luckily for her, the old woman had fallen asleep in the sun reading by the time they returned from the girls' day out.

That's when Pru had disappeared into her attic bedroom. She quickly unwrapped the tissue paper and propped her new purse on her dresser against a stack of books where she'd be able to look at it and admire its beauty. Whether she was going to be brave enough to use it for everyday was still up in the air. She'd likely save it for special occasions—and when Cadence was around to yell at her for not using it.

After one more glance at the pretty new bag, she'd opened the laptop and gone right to work.

She'd already done a deep dive into everything that might be waiting for Cal when he arrived in Apalachin. But she was worried about him being there alone, so she looked one more time for anything she might have missed. She now knew more about the mob in upstate New York than she'd ever imagined there was to know.

Only when she'd exhausted everything she could find on the subject online had she tackled the newest assignment he'd given her.

Narcan. Or, as she'd learned naloxone hydrochloride.

She printed out anything that looked important, feeling guilty at the amount of printer paper she'd used. But somehow, saving it all in a folder on her computer didn't feel good enough.

Once it was printed, she was able to pour over it again, more thoroughly and with a pack of colored highlighters this time. She could connect the dots between seemingly disparate facts more easily when it was in black and white—marked up with pink, green and yellow—on individual pieces of paper.

She stopped short of taping it all to the wall, connected by strings and marked with sticky notes— the equivalent of a murder board like she'd seen on TV. But it had been tempting.

After going over the information more than once, she sat and waited. Afternoon tea with Myra and Cadence was a short but unsatisfying distraction.

Then she was back to waiting, alone while Cadence took a nap and Myra claimed to be reading her book but was most likely also napping.

Pru planted herself on the front porch where she could see the driveway. Sitting with the folder of research and her cell phone in her lap and her heart in a vise, she waited.

Finally, she saw the old Bronco Cal loved so much —all right, she loved it too.

As it wound its way toward the house, relief hit her. At least he was alive and well and not dead and sunk in the river—swimming with the fishes—by some Apalachin mobsters.

Jumping up, she rushed back inside the French doors, through the living room and to the hall. By the time he'd parked and made his way to the house, she was pacing across the marble entry, anxious for him to get there already and tell her what he'd found out.

"Hey," he said when he opened the door and found her there. His gaze went to her hair. "You got your hair done. It looks good."

"Thanks." She would have eaten up that compliment if she hadn't been so worried about him for hours. But he was home now. She let out a breath as she looked him over.

He seemed unscathed although he looked different. It took her a second to realize he'd cut his hair. And when she looked closer, she noticed that even though he'd left the house with a bit of stubble, now he was clean shaven.

She'd waited for hours, worried, and he'd taken the time to go to a barber?

"How did it go?" she asked, following him as he led the way into the living room. He at least owed her some information in exchange for all her worry.

He bobbed his head to the side as he reached into the bar fridge and pulled out a soda. "It was... enlightening."

"In what way?" she asked, starved for details while he remained miserly with them.

"There are definitely mob affiliations with that cluster of vending machines you found in Apalachin— probably in most of the clusters—but I don't believe that presents a threat to the family or the company."

"Why not? How can it not? Senior is going to turn over those records to the IRS. Al Capone went down because of the IRS," she said, panicked by what she knew from all her research.

"I know. And I relayed that to them."

"You what?" Her eyes opened in shock. He'd

CAT JOHNSON

spoken to the mob directly *and* had told them his father was betraying them?

That settled it. He'd been near too many explosions in the SEALs. He must have some serious traumatic brain injury. What was that disease boxers got from getting hit in the head too many times?

Cal held up a hand. "It's okay. Really. They realized long ago the machines could be compromised. I guess they've moved on to less risky enterprises."

"They told you that?"

"Not in those exact words but yeah. Pretty much."

Still spinning from this information and questioning the portrayal of the mob in every movie and TV show she'd ever seen, she stared at him, open mouthed. "So there's really nothing to worry about from them?"

"I honestly don't think there is. At least not from those guys. There's still that email I found but that could be from a pissed off customer for all we know." Cal leaned forward. "Actually, I think the head guy in Apalachin had a crush on Grams."

"What?" Her voice squeaked as much from what he'd said as from his sudden close proximity to her.

"Yeah." He nodded. "He couldn't stop talking about her."

"Really?" Could this whole thing get any stranger? And was Cal going to get any closer?

Pru let out a short nervous laugh. "That's great. Uh, not the crush thing but that we don't have to worry."

"I agree. And I guess Linda's woo-woo prediction was a little off base this time. But don't tell my grandmother I said that." He leaned in conspiratorially and smiled at her.

That smile lit not only his face, but her whole world. With Cal around everything seemed brighter. And with him standing so close, leaning so low, it felt as if maybe there might be hope for something more between them.

But it was all a bit overwhelming. She tried and failed to hold his gaze.

"What's that?" he asked, tipping his chin towards the folder still clutched, forgotten, in her hand.

Happy for the break in the intensity of his stare, she said, "Oh. That's my Narcan research."

"It's, uh, girthy," he said, eying the thick folder.

"I wanted to make sure you had everything you needed."

"Thank you." He tipped his head. "Want to lead me through it?"

Yes. She'd lead him. Or follow him. Or do just about anything he wanted.

Swallowing, she said, "Sure."

Laying the folder on the only area of the bar not crowded by bottles and glassware, she opened it to reveal the first page. He moved up closer behind her, his height making it easy for him to read over her shoulder.

Very conscious of how near he was, she cleared her throat and began. "Opiant Pharmaceuticals developed the Narcan nasal spray and got it approved by the FDA. It's distributed through one of their partners in the US and Canada. And it's now available for purchase over the counter and stocked by the major pharmacy chains. But it's pricey."

"How pricey?" he asked.

"About seventy dollars for a single dose, but they sell it in two dose packages for one-forty because sometimes one dose isn't enough. However, Teva, an Israeli company, and Sandoz, another generic brand manufacturer, both developed generic versions that cost half as much per dose. And then they were sued for patent infringement. But they won in appeals court."

"Good. So the generic is available in the US?" he asked.

"Yes." She flipped to another page and found what she was looking for. "Sandoz announced the US launch of the generic version in December of twenty-twenty-one."

"Good. A thirty-dollar option is much better for the vending machines than one-hundred and forty."

"I agree. But even better than that, there are a bunch of machines distributing it for free."

"Who's footing the bill for that?" Cal asked.

She ran her finger down the edge of the paper until she hit the blue sticky note and flipped to that page. "California has The Naloxone Distribution Project to reduce opioid overdose deaths through the provision of free naloxone."

Pru flipped to another page.

"And nationally, the Substance Abuse and Mental Health Services Administration or SAMHSA administers the Substance Abuse Prevention and Treatment Block Grant or SABG." She glanced over her shoulder at Cal. "Basically, organizations dedicated to the treatment or prevention of substance abuse can apply for a grant to be used for whatever they deem fit—including purchasing Narcan to be distributed for free."

He'd been leaning low, reading the folder over her shoulder. It put him so close, she could feel his breath on her skin.

At least one of them was breathing. She was having

trouble drawing breath with him so near. He was so close she could see the gradation of dark to light blue in his eyes.

"Good job, Pru." He smiled and it stole what little breath she had left.

"Uh, thanks."

"Surprise, big brother. I'm home!"

The interruption startled Pru out of her love-induced stupor.

Cal straightened immediately. His mesmerizing blue gaze that had been focused on her and her research before, turned toward the doorway.

"Cadence." His smile now was for his sister alone and Pru felt the loss of it immediately. As if all the warmth had been sucked out of the room.

He strode toward the willowy blonde who had model-worthy mile-long legs and unattainably perfect hair that belonged in a shampoo-commercial. Pru's ideal. What she wanted and would never have. Thank God they were siblings. Pru would never have a chance if she was up against Cadence for Cal's affection. Not that she had much of a chance anyway.

Cal wrapped Cadence in his arms in a long, strong hug.

As Pru stood, forgotten in the corner of the room, she would have given anything to trade places and be the one in his embrace. But of course, that had only happened once and then only because her parents had just died.

Cadence was her best friend. Her only friend, really. But right now, Pru would have been happier if she'd just go away.

CHAPTER SEVENTEEN

P ru and Cadence exchanged a few words, then Pru excused herself, saying she had to go check on his grandmother.

That left Cal alone with his sister.

He watched Pru pull the door shut behind her before he asked, "You and Pru are still close?"

"Yes." Cadence nodded, taking the soda can right out of his hand. She took a sip and made a face.

"Even with you being away and her here?" he asked.

What was he hoping for? That they weren't still friends so that his thinking naughty thoughts about his little sister's bestie would be slightly less weird?

"Pru and I text all the time. Which is more than I

get from you." Cadence shot him a glare before moving toward the bar.

As she perused the many bottles, he dropped his chin to his chest, guilt hitting him one more time. "I know. I'm sorry. I'll try harder to keep in touch."

After pouring the remainder of his cola into a glass and adding a liberal splash of dark spiced rum to it, she glanced over her shoulder and cocked up a blonde brow. "You'd better."

He watched as she added an ice cube, took a sip of the drink and nodded approvingly at her concoction.

"So, you're legal to drink now, huh," he observed.

"Yes. For like two years. But I guess you forgot that since you *missed* my twenty-first birthday. I wasn't even away for it, Cal. I was here, home, but *you* were not." She emphasized that last part by pointing to him with the hand that held her drink before she took another sip.

He couldn't exactly tell her that he'd had a good excuse for not being home for her birthday. That things were getting pretty hot with Iran during that particular moment in time.

Hell, all of that year had been contentious between the two countries, but the month of her birthday things had gotten so hot the team had been ordered to remain within an hour of base in case they got spun up.

But even if he could have told her all of that, it didn't matter. Because even if he hadn't been on standby, he wouldn't have flown home anyway. Over the past five years, since his last trip home, his efforts to avoid his father trumped his desire to see his sister or his grandmother. It was a sad truth that he had to face, accompanied by the guilt he carried.

"I sent a gift," he said for lack of anything else to say in his own defense.

"You sent a gift *card*, but whatever. I would have rather had my big bro here with me."

"For your big night of legal debauchery at the college bars?" he said trying to lighten the mood.

"Exactly." She smiled. "It's okay. I had Pru with me."

"As designated driver?" He could picture Pru being the steady, responsible one to balance his sister's party girl tendencies.

"Hell no. We ordered a car so she could drink with me. Her twenty-first birthday was right before mine."

"That's right. I'd forgotten Pru is almost exactly your age." No, he hadn't. It was the thing that haunted him at night every time he thought about Pru.

"What's with all this talk about Pru?" Cadence asked as a frown creased her young, flawless brow.

Shit. Busted. Thinking on his feet, he scrambled for a believable excuse. "Nothing. It was just weird when I came home and found her living here."

"Why? She moved in years ago when her parents died."

"Yeah, but I didn't think she'd still be here now."

"Honestly, Cal. Where else could she go with no money? Uncle Guy wasn't exactly raking in the dough as factory floor manager. He'd racked up some credit card debt. Nobody really realized that until Dad went through his accounts after he and Pru's mom both died. There was no life insurance policy. There's a small trust for Pru, and I mean small, but thanks to whatever boilerplate trust form his lawyer used it's locked down until Pru turns twenty-five. If it was meant to be her college fund, that plan failed. Dad had to pay for her tuition."

"Which he no doubt bitched about loud and often." Cal scowled.

Cadence nodded. "She ended up working on campus to earn some cash to pay for her own expenses. Food on campus, textbooks, the gas for your Bronco so she could commute."

That tidbit got his attention. "Pru used my Bronco?"

"Yeah. Dad told her to. He said he wasn't buying

her a car and she wasn't taking Grandma's Mercedes. Didn't you know?"

"No." He scowled, not because Pru had used his Bronco—he was happy she had the option—but because his father had assumed he could tell her to without even asking him.

"Show a little pity, Cal."

Cadence must have seen the displeasure on his face and assumed he was upset with Pru, which he most definitely was not.

"I can't even imagine how horrible it is for her to be completely dependent on our family for everything," she continued. "Just try to be nice to her, okay?"

"I *am* nice to her. I'm nice to everybody."

"Except Dad." She shot him a look as the corner of her mouth quirked up.

He had to give her that one. "I only give him back what he gives to me."

"You're right. He hasn't always been nice to you. But he's pretty horrible to Pru most of the time and she can't run away to California and join the SEALs like you did."

Maybe not that, but she could—she should—leave this town. Figure out who she was and what she wanted to be, aside from his grandmother's dependent. Or assistant, or whatever they were calling her position here.

"She's had a crush on you forever, you know." Cadence donned a devilish expression and broke into his thoughts.

"Pru?" he asked, surprised. And not in a bad way. Her interest in him put a whole new spin on his interest in her.

"Yes. You didn't notice?" Cadence laughed. "Men are so clueless."

"I'm not clueless." He was very observant. It was part of the job. But Pru was so quiet, reserved, and she always had been.

How exactly could he know what she was thinking? She barely even made eye contact with him when she was younger. She always walked around with her head down, fading into the background most of the time. Now wasn't all that much different.

Not sure he believed what Cadence said, he shook his head. "No. You're wrong."

"I am not wrong. Trust me. Now, make yourself a drink and then tell me about what you've been up to in California," she said, changing the subject away from one that was too complicated for him to think about here and now anyway.

He shook his head. He couldn't tell her most of

what he did, but he would take her suggestion about a drink.

Moving to the bar he said, "Nothing interesting to tell. Why don't *you* tell me what you've been up to in—where the fuck are you now? Ithaca?"

She grinned. "Yes. It's a really cool college town. You should come visit. I'm going to be there for another year."

"Another year? So what, you're just going to keep going to college for…ever? How long are you planning to stretch this thing out? As long as Dad will keep paying?"

"Nooo," she said, stretching out the word in her displeasure. "It's a two-year MBA program, smartass. At an elite ivy league university. I'm right on schedule." She scowled at him.

"Mm-hm. So it has nothing to do with you avoiding entering into the real world?" He heard the words that had just come out of his mouth and felt every one of the years that separated him and his sister in age—times two. Christ, he hoped he wasn't turning into his father.

Cadence let out a humph. "The real world is overrated."

After living—and fighting—in some of the worst

places in the world for over a decade, he had to agree...even if this wisdom did stem from his little sister.

CHAPTER EIGHTEEN

P ru heard her name mentioned and paused with
her hand still on the knob of the closed door.

Eavesdropping had never yielded anything but
pain in the past, but Cal was talking about her to her
best friend. She'd want to hear this. Right?

Snippets reached her ears. It started out all right,
but soon she realized she'd been mistaken. So very
mistaken. She did not want to hear this. One thing was
more horrible than the last.

*It was just weird when I came home and found her
living here.*

I didn't think she'd still be here now.

Honestly, Cal. Where else could she go with no money?

This was bad. So bad. Was this what Cal really
thought about her being here in spite of how friendly

he'd been? Why was he even being nice to her? Was it all fake?

She was shaking and blinded by tears and horror as she backed away.

Desperately afraid they'd open the door and find her there, and equally as desperate to get as far away from Cal as she could, she turned and ran. Taking the stairs as fast as she could and covering her mouth to hold in the noise of her sobs the whole way, she was winded by the time she reached her third-floor bedroom.

She sobbed for a good long while, crying herself into a headache. Even when her tears dried, the pain remained. Which only brought the tears back to her hot swollen eyes.

There was no way she could show her face downstairs for dinner. She'd just have to make an excuse and skip it.

She was thirsty from all the crying but definitely not hungry. She was too upset to eat now and besides, they'd had a big late lunch out.

Glancing at the nightstand, she reached for last night's glass of water and downed the tepid liquid. Next to the glass was her cell phone. She picked it up, managed to focus her eyes enough to see to text and sent Cadence a message.

Migraine. Lying down. Not having dinner. Apologize to Myra for me.

It wasn't really a lie at all. Just staring at the letters on the screen had intensified the pain behind her eyes. She actually did what she'd said she was going to. She laid down in her bed, covered her eyes with her forearm to block out the late afternoon sunlight and tried to sleep.

She must have succeeded. She didn't know how much later it was when a soft knock sounded on her door.

No one knocked on her door. Like ever. Cadence would just walk in when she was around. The house staff waited for her to be downstairs before coming in to change her sheets once a week. She handled the general cleaning of her room herself and did her own laundry. And she didn't think Myra or Calvin Senior had ever stepped foot in her room. Or on this floor even.

That left only one person and the thought of that had her frozen.

The knock came again, just as softly as the first, before the door eased open and Cal peeked in. "Hey. Just checking that you're okay. You missed dinner. And another round of my father being passive aggressive, which is always fun."

She swung her legs over the edge of the mattress and stood. "Uh. Yeah. I'm not feeling well."

That was no lie. Seeing him and remembering what she'd overheard had her stomach churning.

To her horror, the memory brought the tears back to her eyes.

"You're crying." He crossed the room in a few strides, his long legs eating up the minimal distance.

"No, I'm not. It's, um, allergies. The landscapers mowed today. That must be what gave me a headache—"

"Stop bullshitting me, Pru and tell me what's really wrong." He towered over her, so tall and broad. Strong. Powerful. Rich. Confident. Without a worry in the world because he was a natural born Swenson. And she was the pitiful poor relation who'd never asked to be made a Swenson in the first place.

Suddenly she was less sad and more mad. Her breath coming fast now, she lifted her chin, looked him straight in the eye and said, "I heard what you said."

"What did I say? When?" Frowning, he looked genuinely confused.

Of course he did. He'd never imagine she'd been listening. They always forgot she was there. Her dullness faded so easily into the background compared to the shine of the Swensons' lives.

"I overheard you talking to Cadence in the living room. You said you didn't know why I was still living here. That it was weird."

He pressed his lips together as he drew in a deep breath that expanded his chest until it looked impossibly broader. Finally, he nodded. "I did say that. Do you want to know why?"

"I know why," she said, accepting it all. It wasn't like she'd ever felt truly welcome. She should have known Cal was just like the rest. "I'm an outsider. An interloper. The poor relation. Even Cadence agrees. She just has pity on me rather than disdain like your father."

And you...

"No, Pru. I said that because I'd gotten caught by my little sister asking too many questions about her best friend and I didn't know what else to say."

She eyed him, gauging his sincerity, but still confused. What was he saying? "I don't understand."

"I like you, Pru. A lot. Too much. Definitely more than I should, considering..."

"Considering what?" she prompted when he left the sentence trail off, her heart pounding. Was he saying what she hoped he was saying?

"Considering you're practically my sister," he continued.

She let out a short laugh. "No. Not even close. Your father would strongly disagree with that and for once I'd agree with him. My mother married your father's cousin. That's barely related by marriage and definitely not by blood."

"You grew up in my house," he pointed out.

She shook her head. "Not until after you no longer lived here."

"You're seven years younger than me," he said.

"Six...and a half," she corrected. She knew the exact number of months and days that comprised that *half* a year but kept that information to herself since it sounded a bit stalkerish.

"You're my sister's best friend." He sighed, as if that was the worst thing in the world.

"So? Did she say anything about you and me?"

You and me. Holy smokes, was there a *you and me* when it came to her and Cal?

How could there be? He was fighting this so hard, coming up with any excuse he could think of. That was not how a man who was really interested acted.

When a man wanted a woman, he moved heaven and earth to be with her. No matter what. It didn't matter how many obstacles were in the way. Real or imagined.

Cal was doing the opposite. He was the one tossing out the roadblocks between them.

She turned to face the wall before he saw the tears that threatened again, so near the surface.

He came up behind her. "Don't turn away."

"Then don't make me cry." She was past trying to lie to him.

"Shit." He mumbled the curse then spun her to face him and pulled her into the solid warmth of his arms.

Suddenly she was eighteen again, on the day of the funerals, and Cal was holding her. Comforting her. Right before he walked away and abandoned her. Never to return until now, five years later.

"Do you know why I left that day? The day of your mom's funeral?" he asked, almost as if he could read her mind and knew what she'd been thinking.

He'd been so drunk that day she'd wondered if he even remembered being here with her.

She pulled back enough to look into his eyes. "No. Why?"

He let out a bitter laugh and shook his head. "I was getting a fucking hard-on from holding you. Your mother had just died. You were crying your eyes out. Your whole life—your entire future—had been turned upside down and I got a hard-on from holding you while you cried."

She wasn't sure what to say to that. She wanted to tell him it was okay. That she'd wanted him to hold her and do so much more that day. Had hoped and dreamed about it.

But she got it. Understood his horror. Nobody had been able to be around her after the accident. She made everyone uncomfortable back them. She still did when it came to certain members of the family.

"I'm sorry." It was all she could come up with to say.

He shook his head. "Why are you apologizing?"

"I don't know."

He scowled. "I want you to stop apologizing. To everyone but in particular to any Swenson. You hear me?"

She wanted to ask why but instead said, "Okay."

He reached up and brushed some residual moisture from her cheek and every nerve ending in her body went on high alert. Her gaze met his and she forced herself to not look away when the intensity got scary.

"Don't look at me like that," he said in a tone that was almost pleading.

"Like what?" she asked still holding his gaze.

"Like you'd do anything I asked of you."

"What would you possibly ask of me that I shouldn't do?" Her mind went to the customer list she'd secretly downloaded from Myra's computer and realized she'd already done such a thing.

But gazing up at Cal as his nostrils flared and his gaze dropped down and then up her body, she had the feeling he wasn't thinking about Swenson Corp. This was more personal.

"There's plenty you shouldn't do. *We* shouldn't do…together," he mumbled as he took a step back and drew in a deep breath. He shook his head as he wiped a hand down his face and mumbled, "Fuck."

"Cal."

"Yeah?"

"Do you want to kiss me?" She couldn't believe she'd had the nerve to actually ask that. It was like she was a new woman. Emboldened. The more uncomfortable Cal became, the more confidence she gained.

"Yes," he admitted, looking pained to do so. Even if he hadn't answered, the hard length clearly outlined, straining the zipper of his shorts, told her the answer.

He was too tall but he was strong and had the reflexes of a SEAL, so when she surprised him by jumping up and wrapping her arms around his neck and her legs around his waist, he caught her.

It was a risk. He could easily dump her on her butt and storm out in horror. But he didn't. When she leaned in and pressed her mouth to his, he sucked in a sharp breath and then forced his tongue between her lips.

The kiss went from zero to intense in seconds. Like a dam bursting when a trickle turns into a deluge and there's no holding it back.

Cal kissed her like he'd been holding in the desire to do so forever and now that he was—kissing her—he wasn't about to stop.

If she wasn't so amazed and in shock that this— everything she'd dreamed of—was really happening, she would have felt the same as he did. This was perfect and she never wanted it to end.

CHAPTER NINETEEN

"We can't do this," Cal gasped when he could bring himself to break away from Pru's mouth.

"Yes, we can."

She was nothing if not persistent. "We *shouldn't* do this," he clarified.

"Why not?" she asked. "And you're not allowed to repeat any of those bullshit excuses from before."

He breathed in and realized he had nothing. All he could do was shake his head.

"Cal."

"Yeah," he answered, feeling much too miserable considering he had Pru beneath him on her bed and her hand was currently cupping his hard-on through his cargo shorts.

"Don't freak out, but I'm doing this." As she said it, she popped the button then lowered the zipper on his shorts.

He groaned but wasn't sure if it was from the desperation of him wanting her to go on or to stop.

She reached inside his boxer briefs and stroked his length and God help him he didn't stop her. Instead he absorbed all the sensations caused by her smooth warm hand gliding over him.

"Roll over," she ordered, being uncharacteristically bossy.

Where was the demure girl he used to know, who liked to sit in the corner and fade into the woodwork?

When he didn't move right away, she gave him a little push.

He lost his balance, knocking him off the one elbow he'd been propped up on to keep his weight off her. He toppled onto his back on the narrow mattress next to her.

"That's better," she said, moving down his body.

"What are you going to do?" He asked the ridiculous question as she gazed up at him from between his thighs.

"What do you think?" The rhetorical question was delivered with an attitude she'd never shown before.

He swallowed. "Pru—"

The protest never made it out of his mouth as she slid her lips over him. A shudder ran through him and he dug his fingers into the bedding to stop himself from fisting her hair and driving himself into her throat.

Kissing her was bad enough, but he would have been able to walk away feeling okay about that if that was all that it had been.

But this… Neither one of them was walking away unscathed from this. This was going to change things.

And God help him, he wasn't doing a damn thing to stop her. In fact, he widened his legs and shoved his shorts lower to give her better access to his cock, because that's the kind of shithead he was.

But Christ did this feel good. Too good. And he knew this wasn't going to be enough. As he forced his eyes open and watched her take him into her mouth, he knew that for certain. And when she opened her eyes and held his gaze while she sucked him off, he felt himself lose more than just his control over his dick.

"Pru, I'm gonna—" His potential warning was cut off by a groan as she doubled down with her hand and mouth.

That was it. He was done. It had been a long sexless deployment followed by the long journey back to

California and his mad dash across the country to get home for his grandmother.

He hadn't even handled things in that area on his own in far too long. His deprived body was primed and ready and what Pru was doing to him felt too good. Resistance was futile.

The point of no return sent shockwaves through him and all he could do was hang on for the ride. He reached for her head but forced his hands away, back to the bed where he gripped the sheets for dear life and came hard.

He kept his mouth clamped shut but couldn't control a deep, near feral groan. He was panting and breathless by the time the last spurt of his release hit the back of her throat and she finally eased off him.

Cal kept his eyes closed, and his arm thrown over his face as he tried to wrap his head around what he'd just let happen. With Pru!

Yes, he was attracted to her. Yes, he wanted her. But to act on that desire when he'd just gotten home and when he was leaving again in just a few short weeks— He shouldn't have let it happen.

"Was that okay? Did I…do it right?" she asked with a stuttering hesitancy that was a complete one-eighty from the woman she'd been just moments before.

Now she was shy and insecure? After he'd just lost his mind from what she'd done to him.

He lowered his arm and forced himself to look at her. The evidence of what they'd done was visibly obvious. All the markers were there. Her eyes were bright. Her cheeks pink. There was a glistening of saliva on her lips before she ran a hand over her mouth.

The smell of sex hung in the air. But more than all of that, he focused on what he saw on her face, beneath the surface. Doubt.

There was an underlying doubt there and it made him want to ease her mind. "Pru, it was *way* more than just okay."

A small smile bowed her lips as her gaze dropped away. And damned if he didn't start to get hard again.

"Pru?"

"Yeah?" When she barely raised her eyes to answer, he cupped her cheek in his palm and made her stop hiding her face by looking down.

He drew in a breath. "You said six and a half years between us?"

She smiled fully now. "Yes."

What he started to do in his head could only be called *sex math*. Because he was having trouble with her being only twenty-three when he was turning thirty this year. If he'd could honestly claim twenty-nine he might feel better about things happening between them, but that big three-oh loomed too close.

His mind kept going back to the last time he was home. When she had just turned eighteen and was still in high school, and he was twenty-four, going on twenty-five with five years in the Navy under his belt. That age gap had felt huge.

He forced himself to think ahead to when the span wouldn't seem so unbreachable.

"So when you're the age I am now, I'll be—"

"Old," she suggested.

"Thirty-six, smart ass." He couldn't help but smile.

"Why are you worrying? I'm more than old enough to drink and drive and… join the Navy if I want to."

"You're not joining the Navy." He had enough to worry about already. "It's just…"

"Just what?"

"You're Pru."

"And you just came in my mouth," she said, matter of factly.

"Jeezus." He covered his face at that cold hard truth.

She pulled his hands away so she could see him. "It's okay. I wanted you to. But I'm going to get naked now."

Shit. That had to be a hint. It was getting late. She

probably wanted to shower, put on PJs, and get to bed —without him there in it with her.

"Oh. Okay. " He pulled up his briefs and yanked the sides of his shorts together to be able to raise the zipper over his growing hard-on. "I'll get out of your way—"

"Cal. Don't you dare leave," she said as she scooted to the end of the bed and stood, keeping her gaze on him, as if making sure he wasn't going anywhere.

Standing there, she did exactly as she promised. She started to strip, pushing her pants down her legs and stepping out of them.

As he watched, he dropped his hands away from the button at his waist and shook his head. "What happened to you?"

"What do you mean?" she asked as her shirt dropped to the floor.

"How did you go from shy one minute to a seductress the next?"

"You said you liked me." She was down to only a bra and underwear now.

"I can't be the only man to say I liked you."

"Your grandmother's ladies charity group isn't exactly a hopping place to meet guys," she joked.

"I mean in high school. College. You must have had boyfriends. Dated."

Still covered by the bra and underwear, thank goodness, she shook her head. "No."

"Why not?"

She lifted one bare shoulder. "I guess because... they weren't... you."

The bravado dropped away and he saw the insecurity in her come forward again. She crossed her arms over her chest, as if second guessing this whole thing.

Damned if Cadence wasn't right about Pru's feelings for him. She'd been into him for a long time. And he'd thought of her as his little sister. Cadence was right about that too—men were clueless.

"Come here." He tipped his head and patted the mattress next to him.

This little interaction had convinced him of a few things. First, if he rejected her now, even if it was for noble reasons, it would crush her. Second, he'd bet money he was her first for all this, which explained her asking if she'd *done it right*. And finally, he didn't have to take this all the way to prove to her she was an amazing, desirable woman that any man, including him, would lose his mind with wanting her.

She moved closer and tentatively sat on the edge of the mattress.

"Lay down," he said.

She did, a dichotomy of sweet and sexy that was sure to fuck with his mind when he left this room later. How much later was up to her.

He ran one fingertip along the waistband of her boy short-style underwear. "If at any time you want me to stop, you just say so. Okay?"

She nodded.

It wasn't good enough. "Say it, Pru. I want to make sure you believe it."

"If I want you to stop, I'll say so…but I'm not going to." She stared at him with sincere guileless eyes.

Not loving that answer, he scowled, He was a man with fifteen years of sexual experience—he'd started when he'd been way too young. And she was a freaking virgin.

He batted back the purely male pride, the feeling of satisfaction of being her first—her only—for anything that happened between them. Then he considered the grave responsibility of his position more seriously.

"We'll see," he said and hooked two fingers into her waistband. He pulled those pale pink panties over her hips, down her legs and all the way off.

As he did, he studied her face. Waiting, watching, worried… Until she slid further down onto the pillow and spread her legs wide for him.

For only him.

CHAPTER TWENTY

"You don't have to kiss me. I mean, I understand if you don't want to," she said, covering her mouth with her fingertips and very aware that she hadn't brushed her teeth after…what she'd just done with him.

"Fuck that." Cal pulled her hand aside, leaned down and covered her mouth with his, thrusting his tongue between her lips. Ignoring what they'd just done.

She was trying not to be self-conscious—and failing at it—until he ran his hand down her bare stomach. Then lower.

The blunt tips of this thick fingers connected with her core and thoughts of her potentially bad tasting mouth fled.

A jolt of pleasure sparked through her but it didn't even begin to satisfy the yearning within her.

Her body craved Cal's touch. More than that, she wanted him. All of him. Not just his fingers…although what they were doing to her felt pretty amazing.

She wanted more. So much more.

Again it was like he read her mind. He slid down her body, his eyes on her the entire time as he positioned himself between her spread thighs, lowered his head and touched his tongue to the spot that had her gasping. His tongue felt amazing, but she didn't really know what amazing was until he slid two fingers inside her.

The feeling of finally being filled had her muscles clenching, wanting more. He worked her with hand and mouth until she couldn't keep her eyes open. Couldn't stop her hips from rising as if on their own.

And when his fingers inside her hit one spot and he doubled down with the pressure of his mouth, there weren't words to describe the wave of ecstasy that washed over her. Not that she would have been able to form words. The only thing she could manage were sounds that weren't even close to the English language.

She must have been loud. Dangerously so since the family bedrooms were directly below hers.

Cal reached up with his free hand and clamped it over her mouth, but he didn't stop what he was doing. And the spasms wracking her body, rhythmically clenching her muscles, squeezing his fingers, pulsing against his mouth, didn't stop either.

Not for a long while.

Finally, pleasure became almost pain. Too intense. Frightening in the potential that she could lose control completely. She reached down with both hands and pushed his head away.

Grinning, he sat up and wiped the back of one hand across his mouth. "I'm not gonna ask if I did that right."

Her face heated and he reacted. Leaning over her and bracketing her face in both palms, he pinned her with his gaze.

He spoke close, right in her face, as he said, "Don't you dare get embarrassed. I loved every fucking second of that. You hear me?"

She nodded.

Looking satisfied, he pressed a kiss to her lips and groaned.

"You're gonna have to deal with me tasting like you," he said before he shoved his tongue into her mouth.

She loved his mouth on hers. Loved even more the

feel of his weight pressing her into the mattress. And the outline of the hard length she felt against her through his shorts.

The only problem here was that he was still dressed. But she could fix that. She reached down and tried to wiggle her hands between their bodies.

Cal pulled back. "What are you doing?"

"Trying to unzip your shorts."

"No." He shook his head and sat up.

"You don't want to…you know?"

"I most definitely want to. But not now. Not tonight. We have time. I'm not leaving New York anytime soon."

"Are you sure?"

He raised a brow. "You have my return flight agenda."

"Yes, but… what if you have a fight with your father or something?"

He smiled. "Even my father at his worst won't be enough to make me leave early. Not this time."

With that assurance, Cal stood, moved toward the door and reached for the doorknob but she wasn't ready to let him go just yet.

She slipped her legs over the side of the bed and grabbed an oversized T-shirt off a chair. Throwing it on, she dove for him at the door.

"Good night kiss?" she asked hopefully.

His lips twitched. "Okay."

Reaching down, he hoisted her up. She wrapped her arms and legs around him and pulled his neck until he was in kissing range.

Their lips met and he didn't hold back. Taking her mouth with his tongue again and groaning when she met him thrust for thrust with her own.

He pulled back, still holding her, and drew in a breath. "If we don't stop this, I'm not going to be able to leave."

"So?" She didn't see anything wrong with him staying all night. Up here in her bedroom, who would know?

He shook his head and smiled. "To be continued."

"Promise?"

"I promise."

"Okay." She unwrapped her legs from his hips and he eased her down until her feet hit the carpeted floor.

With one last glance at her behind him, he shook his head and smiled. "Get some sleep, Pru. I'll see you in the morning."

"And tomorrow night?"

He drew in another breath and nodded. "And tomorrow night."

"Okay. Good night."

"Good night, Pru."

This time he actually made it out the door, but that didn't mean she could sleep.

Her body might be relaxed and her headache was long gone, but her mind was spinning. The memories of being with Cal were too good to shut down for sleep when she couldn't guarantee she'd dream of him.

Who needed dreams, anyway? She had memories now instead.

A loud rumble from the vicinity of her stomach reminded her of what she did need. Food. She'd skipped dinner.

Luckily she was very experienced in sneaking downstairs for a midnight snack. She'd been doing it long enough.

Wondering what leftovers she'd find, she threw on a pair of shorts and a sleeping bra beneath the large T-shirt, and then made her way down the staircase. Her bare feet felt the cold of the marble floor below. Swinging herself around toward the kitchen door with one hand on the bottom of the banister, she was ready to raid the fridge when she heard a noise.

She stopped dead and listened.

The only illumination was from the small picture lights that were left on day and night to illuminate the paintings in the hallway. The brass fixtures above the frames provided enough light for her to walk without turning on more lamps.

The semi-darkness gave her the illusion of being invisible as she crept toward the door of Senior's office.

It could be Cal, doing more snooping. But of course it could also be Calvin Senior and he was the last person she wanted to see. Especially since she was less than presentable. Shorts and an oversized T-shirt and her hair a wild mess from being in bed with Cal was not how she wanted to be seen by his father.

But then she realized, even though there was noise coming from the office there was no light on in there. If there were, she'd see it under the door.

Had Peanut somehow gotten stuck in the office? It wouldn't be the first time the little dog had gone into a room to look out the window or sleep in the sun and one of the staff had closed the door.

That settled it. Senior wouldn't be in there in the dark, but Peanut or Cal might. Figuring it was safe to check which, she eased open the door.

By the time she saw the person with the flashlight standing over the desk someone else had grabbed her from behind.

Her mouth was covered but he couldn't hold both her arms and keep her from screaming and she had both legs free.

She used what she had, kicking backwards while spinning toward him with her free arm out. She tried to hit the light switch and ended up knocking the lamp over before he grabbed her again.

Good. The more noise the better. With that in mind she began to scream behind his hand. It was muffled, but some sound was better than none.

If she could make enough noise someone would hear and come running. Or the thieves would get scared and leave before they got caught.

She kicked out again and this time connected with what felt like his shin. It hurt like hell since she had no shoes on. She could only hope she'd hurt him a little bit.

Maybe if she could get her elbow into his side… But by then his accomplice had made it across the room from behind the desk.

"Hold her!"

"I'm trying."

"Hang on. I'll find something to tie her up with."

"Why don't you have zip ties or something?"

"Because we weren't here to kidnap anybody. We

were just looking for information for now. Something to hold over that bastard Swenson."

Pru stopped struggling. It wasn't doing any good anyway, they still had her completely immobile, and she wanted to hear what they were saying. These weren't ordinary thieves. They weren't here for the art or jewelry or cash.

"Well, I think we've got his daughter, so let's just take her as leverage."

"Good idea."

They were taking her. No! She couldn't let that happen. Every expert said never let them take you to a second location. It was the kiss of death. And she had no intention of dying when things were going so well with Cal.

She fought with renewed energy, kicking and screaming. But with two men holding her, she got a couple of good shots in but couldn't get free.

Changing tactics, she went limp and dropped to the floor like she'd seen protestors do on the news when police were trying to haul them away. She tried to make herself as heavy as possible, dead weight for them to deal with.

God, she hoped she didn't end up dead for real.

She couldn't let them take her.

Diving for the table leg, she grabbed onto it and pulled, sending the piece of furniture topping over. The heavy antique landed on top of her, which minimized the noise and didn't help her cause. But the intruders were talking loud enough maybe someone might hear.

"What's going on here!"

Myra.

Oh, God. Of everyone in this house, why did it have to be Myra who heard and came to check out the noise?

"Fuck. Another one."

"Get her too!"

"On it."

By now Pru's eyes had adjusted to the dim light. And with the door open to the hall, there was enough illumination she could see Myra turn toward the doorway and try to get away.

From her place, captive as she was held immobile against the first intruder's body, she watched the second man grab for the old woman. He managed to get a hold of her shoulder and spin her back. She lost her balance and with a sickening crack, fell and hit her head on the marble door saddle between the hall and the office.

She lay in a heap on the floor.

"Pick her up, put her in the truck and let's go."

"You gonna be able to handle that one alone?"

"If I can't I'll knock her out too."

No!

As they took her—took them both—Pru knew this was it. She was going to die.

And worse than that, she was going to die a virgin.

CHAPTER TWENTY-ONE

C al woke in a particularly chipper mood the next morning. He didn't have to wonder why. He'd slept great. Even later than usual, actually. And the night before with Pru had been pretty amazing.

There was only one thing weighing on him. Just one dark cloud hanging over his otherwise sunny morning.

Cadence.

What would his sister feel about him and Pru becoming—whatever they'd become to each other last night? He'd have to work out what exactly that was later. Right now, Cadence was the priority. Tell her? Or don't tell and keep it a secret—which felt wrong as well as disrespectful to Pru. So if —when—he told Cadence, how would he best do it?

He considered that as he sipped his coffee and waited until his sister finally made her way to the dining room.

The sound of tiny claws on the floor accompanied by human footfalls heralded Cadence's arrival before she actually appeared in the doorway and smiled. "Good morning, big brother."

"Morning," he replied, eyeing his sister to see what kind of mood she was in.

She looked happy. Smiling was good. Her sound of pleasure at finding oat milk next to the coffee urn was another excellent sign, as had been the presence of her favorite breakfast treat this morning—chocolate as well as regular croissants.

Cadence was as happy as she was going to get today. This might be the perfect time to do this. Especially since he'd promised Pru there would be a repeat of last night. He wasn't sure he'd be able to control himself again tonight and stop before they went all the way. If they were going to do this, he wanted to do it with a clear conscience as far as his sister, and Pru's best friend, was concerned.

"Question," he began.

"Answer," Cadence quipped, shooting him a devilish sideways glance.

He pulled his mouth to the side. "Ha, ha."

"Oh, I'm sorry. Weren't we playing word association? I do like to start my day with a brain teaser and I've already done today's Wordle."

Not knowing what this Wordle was and determined not to ask and send them down a rabbit hole and away from the discussion they needed to have, Cal forged ahead. "So, what would you think if— I, uh, asked Pru out?"

Her eyes widened. "Like on a date?"

"Yeah." His heart rate had kicked up as adrenaline hit his bloodstream.

This was ridiculous. This wasn't some life-or-death battle against a terrorist determined to put him and his team in the ground—after parading their bodies online for all to see. This was his little sister and what was on the line was his *sex* life. Nothing more.

Something in the back of his brain niggled uncomfortably. Like an itch needing to be scratched. If he let the thought come to the forefront he realized this could only be about sex. It *couldn't* involve his *love* life—which was non-existent and for good reason.

He couldn't give Pru anything more than his body and his friendship. At least not right now. Not with him in the teams in California and her here, trapped in her bubble under his family's thumb. He couldn't let her make him her whole world. Because if something happened to him... And even if it didn't, the separation would kill her. She felt things deeply. He could see that.

Cadence, on the other hand, had apparently seen no issue with the current situation. She beamed with a smile and actually clapped her hands together. "I think she'd love that. Well, first I think she'd like literally die but after she recovered, I think she's going to be over the moon happy."

Good to hear, though not a surprise after last night. But how Pru would feel hadn't been the question.

"I'm asking how *you'd* feel about it," he clarified.

"I think it's about time." Cadence shot him a glare before tearing off a piece of croissant that didn't have any chocolate on it and slipping it to the dog, who'd settled comfortably in her lap at the breakfast table.

The dog's presence at the breakfast table aside, Cal breathed a bit easier now that the worry about Cadence's reaction had been relieved. Now, he could focus on other things. What would those other things be? Only one word came to mind.

Pru.

Speaking of Pru...

"Where is she anyway?" Cal asked. "She's always been down here already by the time I get downstairs."

"Maybe she slept in. She did have that headache yesterday," Cadence pointed out.

She hadn't looked like she had a headache when he'd left her last night. He kept that to himself, filling his mouth with more coffee instead.

"But I wish Grandmother would get her butt downstairs. We're supposed to do stuff together today," Cadence continued.

"With Pru?" he asked.

"I don't think so." She shook her head.

The image of daytime sex up in Pru's attic bedroom hit him hard, but he squelched it. In what he thought a magnanimous gesture, he said, "Why don't you take her with you? So she feels like part of the family."

He didn't want Pru to feel like an outsider anymore. Or worse, a poor relation slash servant. The kind of person who had overheard him talking about her last night and assumed he didn't want her here.

"All right." Cadence nodded. "If she really wants to go to Grandmother's hair appointment, she's welcome to join us. I figured she'd be happy to have a break since she's the one who takes Grams every week."

"Well, at least ask her."

"Okay. And in fact, looking at the time, I really

should get Grams moving. She's going to have to eat before we leave."

"How about we divide and conquer? You go get Grams moving and I'll check on Pru and see how she's feeling this morning." Mm-hm. Yeah, right. Check on her. Kiss her. Whatever.

"You got it. Meet you back down here for a status report, Captain." The dog held against her hip in her right hand, she delivered a messy salute with her left.

Cal shook his head. "It would be called a SitRep and I'm not a Captain. And please never try and salute like that again."

"Aye-aye, Skipper." She slurped down the last of her coffee while standing, then wiggled her fingers at him in a little wave. "See you in a few."

"Yup."

When she headed for his grandmother's room, Cal took the servants' stairs up to Pru's room. He knocked, twice, but when she didn't answer, he eased open the door and peered inside. The bed was unmade. The light was on. But Pru wasn't there.

She was probably in the bathroom. He moved to the next doorway and found it open and the small room empty. No residual steam from the shower. The towel hanging on the hook was dry. The bristles of her toothbrush felt dry as well. There wasn't even moisture in the sink. No indication that she'd been in there getting ready for the day, which blew his theory that she must have gotten up early and was already out and about on Grams' errands.

So then where was she?

Maybe he missed her. She could have taken the servant's stairs all the way down from the third floor to the kitchen, while he'd followed Cadence up the main stairs and across the second floor to the back stairs.

Pru could be in the kitchen right now. Or, more likely, in the dining room, wondering where he was.

He headed down the back stairs one flight, across the second-floor hall and to the grand staircase. From the top, he saw Cadence already at the bottom. She glanced up as he descended the stairs and said, "Grandma's not in her room."

"Pru isn't in her room either. Could they be somewhere together?" he asked, thinking they should check the garden. Maybe they'd gone for an early morning walk. The one problem with that guess was, Grams was not an early bird.

Cadence shrugged. "Maybe. I don't know. I'll call Pru."

"Good idea." He should have thought of that himself.

Cadence dialed and pressed the cell to her ear. A second later he heard a muted vibration. Immediately on alert, Cal followed the sound and found the source —a cell phone on the floor under the table just outside his father's office door.

Cal stooped to pick it up. The lit display read Cadence's name.

His sister lowered her own cell from her ear and hit to end the call. The phone in Cal's hand went silent.

"This is Pru's cell," he said needlessly.

"Yes, it is. And she's never without it. She even takes it to the shower with her," Cadence confirmed, the concern clear in her expression.

"Call Grams' phone," he said, heart racing.

She shook her head. "That'll do no good. She doesn't carry it. Ever."

Fuck. Cal turned and assessed the situation. Based on its proximity to where he found Pru's phone, his father's office was the first place to start searching for clues.

He opened the door and his heart immediately sank. "Cadence. Call the police."

Instead of doing as he'd asked, she moved up behind him, then sidled past where he blocked the doorway and gasped. "Oh my God. What happened?"

Inside he found a broken lamp on the floor next to an overturned table. *Signs of a struggle.*

The computer usually on his father's desk was gone. *Motive.*

And the pane of glass in the French door nearest the handle was broken out. *Point of entry.*

He bit out an expletive.

"What's happening?" Cadence asked again.

"I can't be one-hundred percent certain but I think Grams and Pru…" He had to swallow away the bile before he could continue. "…have been taken."

"Taken! Taken by who?" Cadence asked.

"I might have some idea. And I know who I should be asking."

And if he was right, he'd been very, very wrong in his assessment of the events of yesterday.

Hopefully not deadly wrong.

CHAPTER TWENTY-TWO

P ru strained against the plastic ties that bound her wrists behind her back. She felt them cutting into her flesh and stopped, trying instead to break her legs loose from where they were secured to the metal cross bar of the chair.

She glanced over at Myra again, ashen and unconscious, the blood drying dark in her gray hair. More concerned for Myra's health than her own safety, Pru glanced at the locked door then started to scoot her chair closer to Myra's.

When she was as close as she could get, their knees touching, she leaned forward and whispered, "Myra. Myra! Can you wake up?"

Please, wake up.

The ramification of Myra never waking hit her

hard. Embarrassed by the mercenary nature of her own thoughts, Pru tried to push aside the thought that if Myra died, so did her security. There'd be no more job. No more free room and board in the Swenson's big house.

But as concerning as that, was that her friend pool, the people who she could count on one hand who loved her, would be reduced by half. From two, Cadence and Myra, to one.

She thought of Cal and how he could be added to that list of people who truly cared about her—and her heart clenched. He'd lose his mind if his grandmother died.

Pru loved the old bird too and she'd be damned if she didn't do everything she could to get them both out of there. Then, once she did, she'd send Cal and his entire SEAL team after whoever these two idiots were who'd dared to take them. And if the SEAL team wasn't available, she'd grab a weapon from Grandpa Swenson's gun cabinet and she and Cal would come after these guys themselves.

She didn't love the idea of hunting animals for sport, but she was completely on board with killing these bad guys. Or at least wounding them—painfully—before turning them over to the authorities.

With her ire up and her determination fueled, she

tried again to wake Myra, knocking into the old lady's knees. "Myra."

She moaned, low and weak. But it proved she was alive. Thank God.

"Can you open your eyes?" Pru asked.

"Why? Do you look any different that I need to see you?" Myra's voice was gravelly. Rough. But her snarky answer was the best thing Pru had heard all day.

"How do you feel?" she asked.

"Like I got hit in the head with a hammer," the old woman answered. Then added, "and like I've been tied to a chair." Her pale blue eyes opened and she blinked against the lights in the room, frowning.

No doubt the brightness wasn't helping her head.

"I'm so sorry," Pru apologized, remembering her promise to Cal about never apologizing to anyone again, especially not a Swenson, and breaking it anyway.

"Why are you sorry?" Myra asked.

"If you hadn't heard me you wouldn't have come in the office. You wouldn't have hit your head. You wouldn't be here now."

"That's ridiculous, girl. They could have come upstairs and gotten me. They could have torched the house. We don't know what they would have done.

But whatever would have or could have happened doesn't matter. We're here now. We have to deal with the cards we've been dealt."

Pragmatic and sharp witted, even now. Pru wished she had half the power to focus the way Myra did.

"Why were they there? What do you think they wanted? They didn't steal anything valuable. Just Uncle Calvin's computer."

"Then that's what they wanted. We were just a bonus, I suppose," Myra answered.

"They think I'm Cadence. I heard them say to take the old man's daughter for leverage," Pru reported. "Leverage for what?"

"For whatever they want my son to do, or to give them."

"Like ransom?" Pru guessed.

"Yes. Or compliance," Myra suggested.

"Compliance?" It seemed a strange word.

What could they want Senior to do that warranted breaking into his home and taking his family? He built vending machines, for goodness' sake.

"I don't understand. What could they possibly want him to do?" Pru asked.

"I think I might know." Myra's voice sounded gruffer the more they talked.

Pru was dehydrated. Myra had to be too. Plus,

she'd lost some blood from the head wound. But there was nothing she could do about it until their captors showed their cowardly selves again and she could beg them for water.

Until then, she was more than interested in what the heck Myra was talking about.

"What do you know?" Pru asked.

Myra glanced at her. This always proud and confident woman, even in this situation, suddenly looked…contrite, for lack of a better word.

"Myra…what did you do?"

"Nothing that I thought would result in *this*. Believe me. I guess I was wrong."

"I think you'd better explain." If she was going to die, she at least wanted to know why.

Myra drew in a breath. "You know my charity group has been focused on the Opioid crisis."

"Yes."

"We decided to spearhead a project. We applied for a grant to start a program to distribute free Naloxone in the Albany area. It seemed a perfect fit. I'd have donated the Swenson vending machines for the distribution. We just needed the product to put inside and approval for the locations."

Naloxone. Vending machines.

It was all too much of a coincidence that Myra had

stumbled upon the exact thing that Senior was currently involved in—a deal with the IRS to get him the Narcan vending machine exclusive contract.

"Did you talk to Uncle Calvin about this?" Pru asked. Starting to fit together the pieces of the puzzle she could see laid out before her.

"Of course. Months ago when the group was putting together the project."

That must have been how Senior got the initial brainstorm to secure a monopoly on the Narcan vending machines by bargaining with the Feds. Information for special treatment. Quid pro quo.

It all made sense now.

But there was still something that didn't track. "Why would that lead to the break-in and us being taken?" she asked.

"We were told that there is already an organization in our region who has the area covered. There were supposed to be free Narcan vending machines already readily available. But our research, and I mean a couple of our members literally went to the locations and looked for themselves, found only one free machine. All the rest were paid."

"Meaning someone got a grant to set up free machines but was earning money on them instead," Pru guessed.

"Exactly. Maybe our application triggered some notification to that other organization."

"Do you have that other organization's name?" Pru asked.

"Yes. But we had just started to try to figure out what to do about it when this happened."

"You have a Navy SEAL for a grandson. Why didn't you say something to him? He could have helped. Or would know who to call." Instead the old women had played detective on their own and look where they'd ended up.

"Cal knew. We were all there the night he found out about his father and the deal with the IRS," Myra countered.

"Yes, but knowing there was some criminal enterprise already set up to take advantage of the Narcan machines would have been helpful. Especially since he went to Apalachin and confronted the mob. What if this is them?"

"Cal went to Apalachin?" Had Myra's eyes gone dreamy? As if she was remembering something or someone fondly.

"Yes. Today… I mean yesterday." The sun had risen. It was officially tomorrow. The day after they'd been taken. Hopefully the day they didn't die.

"Could it be them, Myra? The mob? The ones

running the Narcan machine scam? The ones responsible for…this? Taking us."

She pressed her thin, pale lips together. "I certainly hope not."

"But you don't know?" Pru prompted.

"I don't know," Myra admitted.

The door flung open, banging against the wall and startling Pru into a yelp.

Two masked men carried a third limp figure between them. They dumped him unceremoniously on the floor before pulling down the bandana covering his nose and mouth and slamming the door closed again.

Myra stared at the crumpled person on the floor. "Perhaps he has some answers." She audibly swallowed. "If he wakes up."

Pru couldn't see the face, but she studied the form. The suit. The leather shoes. The watch. Realization dawned slowly, then all at once and she knew with certainty who was on the floor.

They'd just been joined by Calvin Swenson Senior.

CHAPTER TWENTY-THREE

Cal had already lost his cool and was on the way to losing his mind.

He couldn't concentrate. Couldn't focus. All his training went out the window when he realized his grandmother and Pru were gone, likely taken.

There was no compartmentalization in this situation. No separating the mission from his personal life.

He couldn't force himself into warrior mode. He was thinking like Myra's grandson. Like Pru's lover. When what he needed to be doing was thinking and acting like a SEAL.

A SEAL without back up. Without resources.

Fuck.

Think!

"What are we going to do?" Cadence asked, not for the first time.

"Let me think," he said, more sharply than he'd intended. He shouldn't take his frustration out on her. It was himself he was angry at. And the animals who'd done this.

The police had come and gone. They'd told him to sit tight and let them do their job. They were on the case.

Forgive him if he didn't have the confidence they did. Especially since they seemed more focused on the break in and missing computer. He couldn't shake the feeling that, although they promised to fill out a missing persons' report, the cops still felt as if Pru and Myra were just going to stroll in the front door any moment after a shopping spree. Just two self-centered rich people acting eccentric, as usual. In spite of the evidence.

"The intruders could have knocked over the lamp and table," they'd said. "Is it possible Miss Swenson could have dropped her cell on the way out this morning?" they'd asked.

No! Not if his gut instincts could still be trusted.

And through it all, his father was MIA as well. But there was nothing nefarious about his disappearance. The hanger from today's suit hung empty in his closet.

His watch, cell phone and wallet were gone from his dresser, where they lived at night, according to the staff. And his car was gone, just like every morning when he left early for work. Along with the paper they always left for him on the dining room table.

It wasn't even odd that he wasn't answering his cell. According to Cadence, who apparently called him daily, he rarely answered, preferring to return calls later on his own schedule.

Well, *later* might be too late.

"I'm going to the factory." He stood, nearly knocking the dining room chair over in the process.

"Wait. Why? To see Dad?"

"Yes. And to tell him what he doesn't know since he doesn't answer his fucking phone. That his mother has possibly been kidnapped." He answered on his way to the locked gun closet.

He had the door unlocked and open by the time Cadence stepped up beside him, the dog whining at her feet as he sensed her agitation.

"I'm going with you," she said.

"No. Stay here in case the police call." He swallowed hard. "Or the kidnappers." Best case scenario, there'd be a call with a ransom demand and proof of life.

"O—okay." Her eyes widened, he wasn't sure

whether that was from his comment or the Colt .45 in his hand. It was the pistol that his grandfather had taught him to shoot with.

He shoved extra clips into the pockets of his cargo shorts then closed but didn't lock the door so Cadence had access to the three generations worth of weapons if she needed.

Turning back, he saw the panic on his sister's face. He closed the distance between them and wrapped her in a hug.

He blew out a breath. "It's going to be all right."

She pulled back. Her eyes, so like their mother's, gazed up at him. "Do you really believe that?"

"I have to." He released her and took a step back. "I'll call you."

"You'd better," she said to his back as he strode out the door.

The visit to his father's factory told him one thing. All was not well. He might not have logged many hours at this building, but he knew when things were amiss. He didn't even have to go inside to see it.

He'd parked next to his father's Audi in the lot and immediately knew there was a problem. The driver's side door was open. Not unlocked, but actually standing wide open, as if he'd been grabbed while getting out of the car on his way into work this morning.

There was now no doubt in his mind. Pru and his grandmother were not off somewhere together having the time of their lives, like the police had insinuated. Someone was systematically grabbing members of his family.

Cadence.

He whipped the cell out of his pocket and hit to call her phone. She answered on the first ring and said, "What's happening?"

"Dad's been taken too."

"What?" There was panic in the high-pitched reply.

"You need to get somewhere safe."

"I am. I'm home."

"Home is not safe, Cadence. Pru and Grams were home too."

She drew in an audible breath. "Where do I go?"

Good question. The police station? But he didn't want her to leave the house. What was to stop someone from grabbing her from her car like they had her father?

"Change of plans. Stay there. But I need you to gather the staff now. All of them. Tell them what's happening. They need to lock down that house. Every door. Every window. Then I need you to go into

Grandpa's gun closet and arm any one of the staff who has experience with a weapon and is comfortable using it if they have to. No one gets in that house unless it's me. Don't even let the police in. We don't know who we can trust at this point. Got it? Make sure the indoor and the outdoor staff understands that."

"Cal. You're scaring me."

"Good. You need to be on alert. Now listen to me. You're not safe on the first floor. Whoever got in last night did it by breaking a window. So you need to be upstairs. Okay? Take a gun. Whichever you feel most comfortable shooting. Make sure it's loaded. Don't forget to grab extra ammunition. Then go in your room and lock your door."

He didn't worry about giving her that order to arm herself. They'd all had plenty of shooting experience over the years. Skeet. Target. Some of it for fun. Some of it because his grandfather believed gun safety came from knowledge and experience.

"Okay," she said, her voice shaking. "What are you going to do?"

"I don't know yet." *Or maybe he did...*

Getting back into his Bronco, after slamming his father's car door, he said, "Text me every fifteen minutes. Okay? No matter what. If I don't get a text I'm going to assume something happened."

"I'll text you. I promise. I'll set an alarm to remind me."

"Good. I gotta go."

"Cal."

"Yeah?"

"Be careful."

"Yeah." He hung up, not willing to lie to his sister and make promises he wasn't sure he could keep.

His safety was not the primary concern right now, except for the fact that he needed to stay alive and functioning long enough to dispense of whoever had done this and get his grandmother and Pru back.

CHAPTER TWENTY-FOUR

The two-and-a-half-hour drive to Apalachin nearly killed him. Anything could be happening to his family while he was forced to sit behind the wheel of the Bronco, obeying traffic laws.

Obeying some traffic laws, anyway. He certainly wasn't driving the I-88 posted speed limit. It was only the limitations of the aging Bronco that kept him from topping one hundred. Even driving eighty-five felt too slow given the situation and what was at stake.

But this was a trip that had to be made. It wasn't like he could call Rocky's barbershop, ask if Vincent was there and accuse the man of kidnapping his family. He needed to look the man in the eye to know if he was lying, because whether he was guilty or not,

Vincent was certain to deny it. The mob wasn't real into full disclosure and admitting guilt.

So here he went, back to visit with the mob. While anything could be happening to Pru and his grandmother. He felt ill thinking about how scared they must be. His heart pounded considering what could be happening to them right at this very moment.

His father too, although that thought had Cal clenching his jaw in anger. That man and his shortsighted self-centered greed had brought this down on them all.

Cadence's quarter-hourly texts kept him from losing his mind completely and helped break up the long drive. Every text meant he was fifteen minutes closer to his destination, until finally he saw the sign for Apalachin.

He slowed considerably and pulled into town, parking down the block and picking up his phone. He wanted to check in with Cadence before he confronted Vincent. Just in case.

She didn't answer until the third ring, which did nothing for his already ragged nerves.

"Hey."

"Hey." He breathed in relief that she sounded fine. Then he frowned. "What is all that noise in the background? Who's there with you?"

"I called Grandmother's friend Linda to tell her what was happening. I thought she should know. She called their friend Agnes. They both drove right over to help. And then Grams missed her charity group meeting today, so Sue stopped by to check on her. When she heard what was happening, she of course wanted to stay too."

"I told you no one comes inside."

"Cal. They're old family friends. They didn't kidnap Grams and Pru. Or Dad. I think it's safe. And besides, Agnes was in the Army when she was younger. She's like, really knowledgeable about guns. And with you gone, I needed someone here with me. For support."

He sighed, pissed at himself that he hadn't thought what it would be like for Cadence there without him with all this shit happening. "Okay. I'm glad they're there for you. But don't let anyone else in, okay?"

"I won't. I promise. I'm putting you on speaker. They want to talk to you."

"Fine," he said, not believing her promise.

She'd even managed to turn this into a party of sorts. He hoped Agnes was good with a gun, and that she had one with her, since God only knew who could sneak into the house while all that chaos was happening.

"Cal. We think we have some information that might be pertinent to the case," a voice he didn't recognized said.

"That's Agnes, by the way. Grams' college friend from Mudville," Cadence supplied.

God help him. As much as he had mixed feelings about the CIA at times, he'd welcome one of their briefings right now.

"All right. What have you got?" he asked.

"Why don't you explain, Sue?" another voice he didn't recognize said.

"That was Linda, Grams' friend who predicted all this was going to happen," Cadence clarified.

Not exactly. All Linda had done was coincidentally say something bad might happen. But he wasn't going to argue that point now.

"Go on," he prompted.

"Hi, Cal. This is Sue. Your grandmother and our charity group were working on a project. The plan was to provide vending machines to dispense Narcan for free in high-risk areas..."

That captured his attention. Vending machines. His father's deal with the IRS. It all came back to the Narcan.

He listened more closely now as Sue continued, "When we applied for the SABG grant with SAMHSA, we were told there's already an organization in the Albany area doing exactly what we'd planned. They even gave us the locations of these supposedly free machines. But when we investigated, we found one free machine and that all the rest weren't free at all. They were charging one-hundred and forty dollars for a two-pack of Narcan. So we of course are going to send a strongly worded letter to SAMHSA telling them this other organization who was benefiting from the grant, which should be our grant, was not adhering to the conditions they applied under. That's what today's meeting was about. To vote to approve the wording of the letter before we send it off."

His head was spinning. All the acronyms she spouted were so familiar. It took a few seconds before he realized it had all been in Pru's Narcan report to him. The grant. The cost of the name brand Narcan. She'd found it all.

And so had his grandmother's organization. But they hadn't told anyone what they'd found yet. So whoever was running this grant scam shouldn't be aware yet. Unless the women talked to the owner of the machines.

"Sue, did you speak with anyone when you were investigating these paid machines?" Cal asked.

"No. We were careful not to. Once we discovered

there was a scam afoot, we decided to remain undercover."

God save him from a bunch of old women playing sleuth. Unfortunately, Sue's answer blew his last theory.

"But there was one time, I encountered a man filling the machine."

"You did? Did you speak with him?"

"Yes. But I was careful. I pretended I didn't know what the machine was for—no one thinks us mature ladies know anything about what's happening in the real world—so I played dumb and asked what Narcan was and why it cost so much. And the guy filling the machine told me."

"Uh huh." Still not helpful.

"But that's not the interesting part..." she began.

"What was?" he prompted, wishing she'd hurry.

"It was when a guy from Swenson Corp pulled up in a van. He came over and said he was there to service the machine. Said he was changing out the computer chip inside. When the guy filling the machine asked why and told him the machine was operating just fine, that it didn't need repair, the Swenson guy said it was his orders to update every chip in every machine. And that he'd heard a rumor that the updated chip had the capability to remotely deliver reports of earnings and inventory. The Swenson guy said he figured the upgrade was to benefit owners who didn't want to drive around to check the machines. They'd know when they were low on inventory from the reports. The guy filling the machine didn't seem to like that idea. He went pale and then ran off to make a phone call."

Cal had a feeling he might have gone pale himself at this information as they came full circle. Back to his father's deal with the IRS to turn over earnings reports and how it would affect the owners of the vending machines who might rely on that information being untraceable.

He glanced up at Rocky's barber shop, visible down the block through the Bronco's windshield. Vincent had assured him they already assumed the vending machines were compromised, since they were less and less all cash and more and more took debit and credit cards. But whoever was running those Narcan machines must not feel the same.

Were they part of the mob? Did Vincent know who they were? Cal was going to find out.

"All right. Thanks for that information."

"Did it help?" Cadence asked.

He heard the change in the sound level. She must have taken him off speakerphone. "Yeah. It did."

"Oh good."

"Cadie, listen to me. I want you to remember this. I'm in Apalachin, New York. And I'm about to go into Rocky's barber shop."

"To get a haircut? In Apalachin?"

"No. Not to get a haircut. I'm here because I think they might know something."

"You're telling me where you are because you're worried you won't come back," she whispered.

"No. I'm telling you where I am because it's important information you should have. Now repeat what I told you."

"Apalachin. Rocky's."

"Good. I'll call you as soon as I can."

"Okay." There was a tremor in her voice.

She was scared. Good. Maybe she'd be a little more careful and a little less carefree over there with her ladies.

"Love you, bye." He disconnected and put the Bronco into gear, pulling out onto the street to park again one block down, this time directly in front of the barbershop.

If he needed to make a quick escape, he wanted the vehicle close. Cutting the engine, he left the keys in the ignition. No one was going to steal it and those seconds saved not having to get the key in could just save his life.

He got out and stood on the sidewalk staring through the glass door of Rocky's, the weight of the gun in his pocket heavy.

Time to do this...

CHAPTER TWENTY-FIVE

"Look who's back," Rocky said in greeting when Cal opened the door. "You need a shave again already?"

"Uh, no. I'm not here for a shave." He must have telegraphed what he was feeling and thinking because he saw and felt every man in the shop go on high alert. Vito even stuck his hand beneath his suit jacket where Cal had no doubt there was a shoulder holster complete with weapon.

"What do you need?" Rocky asked, far less friendly now.

"Sometime last night our house was broken into. My grandmother and my...cousin Pru are both missing. My father's gone missing as well. Taken from the factory in Albany early this morning as he got out of his car, as far as I can tell."

"You accusing us of having something to do with this?" Vito stood and moved a step closer, his hand still precariously inside his jacket.

"Should I be?" Cal asked, not backing down.

"Watch your tone, boy," Rocky warned Cal.

Vincent, who'd sat and silently watched the exchange until now, held up one hand. "It's okay. He's distraught."

"So? This is about respect and he's not showing any," Vito countered.

"This is about family and family comes first," Vincent corrected. He turned his full attention to Cal. "I'm sorry to hear this. But I swear to you, on my son and daughter's lives, we are not responsible."

Cal believed him. What he wasn't sure of was if he could trust his own instincts right now. He wasn't a warrior SEAL here and now. Wasn't thinking like an experienced operator.

He let out a breath and felt his shoulders sag. Part from relief he wasn't taking on the mob alone. Part from frustrated despair because now he needed a plan B.

Vincent laid a hand on his shoulder. "Sit. Talk. Tell

me what you know. Maybe we can figure this out. Vito, get him some of the good stuff."

Cal shook his head. "No. I can't drink. I have to drive back."

Vincent smiled. "It's espresso. We keep the machine in back. Unless you want a cappuccino instead."

Cal let out a short laugh. "Yeah. Thanks. Espresso would be good." He had a feeling it was going to be a long day…and night.

As Vito grumbled his way to the back to get the coffee, Cal gathered his thoughts.

"They got in by breaking a small pane of glass out of the patio door in my father's home office."

"No house alarm?" Vincent asked.

"Apparently it wasn't turned on." But that complacency was going to change. "I don't know how many men but in the morning I found the furniture in the office overturned and Pru's cell phone under a table in the front hall. Both my grandmother and my cousin are missing."

Cousin was so inaccurate it hurt him to say the word. Besides the fact she was more like his second stepcousin, Pru was so much more than that to him.

"Tell me about your father. You said he's missing too?" Vincent prompted.

"He wasn't answering his phone. Evidence at home

223

suggests he got dressed, grabbed his newspaper and drove to the factory early, before any of the rest of us were up. I went to the factory and found his car parked in the lot and the car door standing wide open. A call to his secretary yielded that she hadn't seen or heard from him this morning."

"You call the cops?" Vincent asked.

"Yes."

"Too bad," Rocky mumbled. And Cal knew why. The authorities being involved limited Cal's choices for COAs—courses of action—to legal means. Or would have *if* Cal was in the mindset to give a fuck.

He shook his head to eliminate Rocky's concern. "That's not gonna matter. I'm going to do whatever I have to do to get my family back."

"That's a good boy." Vincent nodded. "Tell me who you think would do this—besides us."

He smothered a cringe. Yes, he'd just accused the mob of kidnapping without having any real, hard evidence to do so. Luckily, they'd taken it pretty well.

"I think it has to do with the new Narcan vending machines." Cal went on to explain all he'd learned from Sue on the call.

Vincent's eyes narrowed and his jaw got hard. When Cal finished, Vincent said, "You know, some guy approached us about putting one of his machines in our town. We told him we'd put our own damn machine here and we'd stock it with the generic version so that folks who need it can afford it. Not that expensive stuff he was peddling. Don't need him lining his pockets on the backs of our folks."

"Yeah, if anyone's gonna line their pockets, it's us!" Vito said as he dropped the espresso cup onto the table near Cal. "There."

Cal glanced up and said thanks before getting back to the subject. "It's got to be him. Based on what Sue told me, and the fact they stole his computer, this guy is aware my father is capable of turning over evidence of actual income to the IRS. Besides that, he's about to be caught making a profit selling Narcan obtained using a government grant that was meant to provide the product for free."

Rocky nodded. "He's about to go down and he knows it. He might be desperate enough to resort to kidnapping. Demand your father edit those reports to the IRS to exclude his Narcan machines."

"And use your cousin and Myra as leverage." Vincent shook his head. "It ain't right, involving the family when his beef is with your dad. That's something *we don't do*."

"I'm sorry. I didn't mean—" Cal began his apology.

Vincent waved it away. "Forget about it. What are we going to do now?"

"We?" Cal asked.

"You can't go in alone. You don't know what you're facing. And you can't count on the cops. Besides the fact I have no love for cops in general, their hands are tied by the law." Vincent shook his head. "You know, shitheads like these Narcan guys give respectable businessmen like us a bad name. I'm more than happy to loan you a crew to go in and get your family back and teach these guys a lesson."

Cal opened his mouth to protest but they were right. He didn't know what he was facing. And he was without the backup of his team.

But that didn't mean he was completely alone here. He glanced around at the three men. "You would do that? Back me up?"

Vincent nodded. "Anything for Myra and her family."

One day Cal was going to have to investigate that connection, but for now, he needed to figure out where this company was located and where they might stash hostages.

"You guys don't have a computer whizz on your payroll, do you?" Cal asked. "Somebody who could find the addresses of all the properties in the area owned by a shell company?"

Vincent raised a brow. "I've got a pretty creative accountant but I don't think he's got the kind of computer skills you're talking about. Don't you have any connections?" he asked.

Did he? He couldn't call command in Coronado, but there might be someone he could call.

He nodded. "Yeah. I just might."

Zane Alexander had left the teams years ago. He'd been on his way out when Cal was still a newbie SEAL, but the man's reputation and that of his partner Jon Rudnick lived on.

They were stellar SEALs but what they'd accomplished post service was even more impressive. They'd founded one of the most elite and successful PMCs in a country that was already packed with private military contractors. Rumor had it they had more government contracts than they knew how to staff, as well as high value, close personal protection contracts, including for some well-known celebs.

What Cal hoped was that his position as a frogman in need would be enough to get the busy man's attention, and that the Swenson money would secure him the information he needed. But first, he needed a damn phone number.

He wracked his brain, trying to remember the name of the company to no avail. As Vincent made his own phone calls, having much more success rounding up his team than Cal was having gaining the information he needed, he finally resorted to Google.

A search for Zane Alexander and Jon Rudnick brought up articles and photos and news reports of the two and yielded the name of the company. GAPS, short for Guardian Angel Protection Services. And lo and behold, they had two offices on the east coast. One in Virginia Beach and one in the D.C. area, and there were phone numbers listed for both.

He hit the number for one of the listings and a pleasant female greeted him with, Guardian Angel Protection Services, this is Chelsea speaking.

"Chelsea. Hi. I was hoping to get in contact with Zane Alexander."

"Who's calling?"

"Um, Calvin Swenson. He and I were in the SEALs together." That was a bit of a stretch and Zane would no doubt realize that the moment he didn't recognize Cal's name from any of the teams he'd been on during his SEAL career, but desperate times…

"Hold, please." Chelsea hit the hold button, which cued up what was meant to be soothing hold music but instead just ramped up Cal's tension.

"Zane Alexander." The voice of the man himself suddenly in his ear rattled Cal.

It took him a second to regain his composure before he rushed to say, "Hi. Thanks for taking my call."

"No problem. What can I do for you, Calvin?"

"Um, this might be a strange request…"

"I've heard it all. Go ahead. Shoot."

Cal laid the situation out one more time for the SEAL, stressing the unique challenges he was up against. The kidnapping. The police's lackluster response to his missing family members. The evidence they had leading them to possible suspects. And the fact he was on leave and without official resources or support.

"What exactly are you looking for from me?" Zane asked. "I've got some men in New York but it would take some time to get them to you—"

"Actually, I've got backup. I was hoping you could get me information. All I have is the name of the shell corporation that applied for the grant. I need the names of the people behind it and the addresses of any properties they own or lease."

"You're hoping they took your family to one of their properties."

"Yes."

"I don't suppose you're planning on turning that information over to the police."

"Nope." No use lying.

"I'm going to be perfectly honest with you. The number of government contracts we've acquired since opening our D.C. office is staggering. It's also limiting. I've got a computer guy on the payroll. I also have resources that are still active in the Navy I call on occasionally. But I can't have GAPS involved in something like this. You go in, guns blazing, and it comes out that we're the ones who supplied you with the address? That would be the death knell for all our government work."

Cal's chest clenched as his one last hope fell. "I understand. Thanks, anyway."

"Hang on. I said GAPS couldn't help you. I never said I didn't have a resource for you. You didn't hear it from me but occasionally I'm forced to work in the gray areas. And for that, I have a woman on call. Eva Lucas. She's from your area, I think. Skaneateles, New York? Anyway, it doesn't matter. She moved to Bitter End, Tennessee for some unknown reason but she's still taking freelance computer jobs."

"She's good?" Cal asked, not sure about this recommendation.

"Eva's not good. She's the best," Zane said with conviction.

"All right. Can I contact her directly?"

"Yeah. Let me text you her number."

"Thank you. Seriously. I don't know what I would have done."

"You'd have figured it out. Frogmen always do."

Armed with this Eva person's number and still holding on to one last hope, Cal made the call.

It took a few rings and his heart was pounding by the time he heard her say, "Hello?"

"Is this Eva Lucas?"

"Who's asking?" She sounded about as wary as a person who made a living working on the dark web in the gray areas of society would.

"This is Cal Swenson—" he began.

"I don't know any Cal Swenson."

"Zane Alexander from Guardian Angel Protection Services told me to call you. He gave me your number," Cal rushed to add before she hung up on him and his last hope disappeared.

"Jesus. Why didn't you just say that to begin with? What do you need?"

What *did* he need?

He needed Pru back and his grandmother safe. And he really needed to slug his father just once with a good old fashioned knockout punch for making that deal and setting these events in motion to begin with. And he needed any possible location where the sons of bitches who had his family might be hiding them.

That last part was what he told Eva, along with what little information he had to provide that might help with her search.

"I'm on it. My rate's a hundred and fifty an hour plus whatever I pay for information."

"Money is no object."

Eva let out a snort. "Okay, Richie Rich. Stay by your phone. I'll call you back on this number when I've got something."

"How long—" He didn't get the words out before the call went silent. That left him with nothing to do but wait.

Vincent raised his gaze as Cal laid his phone on the table and said, "She's going to call back."

The man nodded. Impeccable as ever in a navy-blue suit, he picked up the tiny espresso cup and raised it to his lips, as calm as ever. No one would ever guess he had a mob hit squad on alert, waiting for his call to go into action.

The seconds turned to minutes which turned to half an hour. Cadence texted to check on him when he should have been checking on her.

Then, finally, the cell rang. Every eye in the shop snapped to the phone as Cal, ignoring the shaking of his hand, hit to put the call on speaker. "Cal Swenson."

"Hey. I got a name and a location. A warehouse property not too far from where you are now. I've texted it to you."

As his cell dinged with the incoming text, those around him sprang into action, Cal swallowed hard as relief and adrenaline collided within him. He stood, but knew he had to finish up business with Eva before anything else. "What do I owe you?"

"I'll text you payment info."

"Thank—"

Again she was gone before he could finish, which was fine. They needed to go.

"What are you carrying?" Vincent asked, his gaze dropping to the telltale bulge in Cal's pockets. Wishing for the kit in his cage back at Coronado—hell, he'd settle for just a holster at this point—he slipped out the gun for Vincent to see, after a glance at the glass door to the street.

Rocky laughed. Vito snorted and Vincent shook his head and smiled. "We can do better than that. Get in your vehicle and follow us."

"Follow you to where?" he asked.

"The armory," Vito supplied.

"And to pick up the last member of our team," Rocky said, flipping the sign on the door from Open to Closed.

The *armory* turned out to be the basement of the beauty parlor Cal had visited that first time. It was where they stored their weapons thinking a shop full of ladies was less likely to get raided than anywhere else.

The feds might underestimate females, but Cal knew better. Especially after today. Eva the hacker. Roseanne, Vincent's ex-wife and the boss who ran this portion of the enterprise out of the beauty parlor. Both were proof that women were capable bad asses.

The armory was surprise number one. Surprise number two was that in the back room of the beauty shop was a raucous card game and signs of a thriving bookie enterprise, judging by the woman on the phone taking a steady stream of calls while jotting down numbers in a notebook.

But surprise number three was the real kicker. The final member of their team was that bookie. Rocky's daughter. Who was also, he was told, a sharpshooter. The best they had.

Cal left the shop armed to the teeth, including body armor, flash bangs, a grenade and a semi-automatic with extra clips, and an odd ball team, all equally equipped.

Zane was right to keep his company clear of this possible clusterfuck in the making. Cal could just picture the story on the local evening news if things went sideways. He'd just have to do everything in his power to make sure they didn't.

CHAPTER TWENTY-SIX

I t had been hours. Exactly how many hours, Pru couldn't tell without benefit of a watch. Or even a window. Or a cell phone—where hers had ended up last night she couldn't guess, but she'd give anything to have it with her. To be able to tell Siri to call the police.

What she did know was they'd been there long enough that she was so thirsty her head hurt.

Her bigger concern was Myra. At seventy-two, Myra's head injury combined with dehydration seemed dangerous. Deadly.

What she was not all that concerned about was Calvin Senior. He'd regained consciousness and immediately started ranting, complaining and yelling with a level of intensity that proved he was definitely not injured.

They'd knocked him out with ether or chloroform or whatever the bad guys had used on the bandana they'd had tied over his nose and mouth when they'd first dragged him in.

The less kind side of Pru wished they'd left the gag on him. His ruckus wasn't helping her head and it couldn't be doing any good for Myra's either.

That was proven when Myra let out a huff. "Honestly, Calvin. Shut up."

Senior's eyes widened at the reprimand from his mother, that in Pru's opinion should have come long ago.

Yes, she was cranky but she had every right.

Her arms were numb from being bound behind her. Despite feeling severely dehydrated she feared she was going to have to pee eventually and couldn't imagine their captors offering to take her to a bathroom.

Then there was the chance they'd just kill them all. Or worse, leave them there to die a slow and horrible death with Senior complaining to the bitter end.

She was running short on compassion for the man since there was a good chance this was all his fault. The fact he'd been taken too just reinforced that theory. They already knew he was playing with fire with that deal with the IRS.

Why else would the family suddenly be a target?

It wasn't like there was a vending machine manufacturing war going on.

She narrowed her eyes and glared at him. It felt so much better to be mad for a moment instead of scared. It might not last long but she'd take what she could get.

The fact she and Myra had chairs and he was just bound and on the floor made her feel moderately better as well.

"What are you staring at?" Senior said, returning her a glare.

She wasn't going to go into battle with the man. She'd witnessed first-hand there was no winning with a man who stubbornly refused to be wrong about anything, even when he so obviously was.

Scowling, she averted her gaze, looking around the room for something, anything, that might help them. Maybe a sharp edge to cut the plastic ties that she could hop her chair over to. If Senior would stop complaining and use his brain for good instead of evil, he could wiggle his way to the door and—

And what? See if the men who'd taken them were

dumb enough to leave it unlocked? It was a long shot but it wasn't like they had anything else to do.

Except wait to die.

She pushed that thought aside and was trying to think of how to ask Senior, in a way he'd listen to her which he rarely did, if he could try to break his ties, when she heard it. A kind of scratching sound from the door.

Her eyes went wide. Were there rats? Were they going to be attacked by starving vicious little creatures with sharp teeth and beady eyes?

With her hands and feet tied she couldn't defend herself. They'd eat her eyeballs first, probably. They were the softest. Juicy and tender.

As thoughts, one more horrific than the last, filled her head, the door swung in.

She almost passed out when she saw four men. They'd multiplied, doubling in number.

They were all in black ski masks. All armed to the teeth with guns bigger than they even had in Grandpa Swenson's gun closet back at the big house.

One seemed to pinpoint her. She could see the moment his blue eyes locked on hers and he began to stride forward, directly toward her.

Her breath coming in quick pants she considered screaming but didn't think there was enough air in her lungs. What good would it do anyway? She was helpless—

"Pru. Jeezus, I was so worried."

"Calvin?" Was she delirious? Was this a fever dream caused by dehydration? "How did you get in here?"

"Vito picked the lock," he answered as he moved behind her.

The tight plastic ties binding her wrists loosened, then the ones on her legs gave way.

Pru felt herself sway precariously almost falling out of the chair as she twisted to look at him.

"Are you all right? Can you walk?" he asked, his hands on her shoulders, steadying her.

"I think so." Her legs were numb but to get out of there, she'd make them work. "Your grandmother—"

Cal glanced up, still in the mask and looking more like a bad guy than a good one. "Vincent's got her."

Who the heck was Vincent? And Vito and the other guy? Were these SEALs? Did Calvin bring in the US Navy to rescue her? As he lifted her from the seat and wrapped her in a tight hard but much too brief embrace, she started to believe he just might.

"Come on. We gotta get out of here."

She wasn't going to argue with that.

Two men had Myra between them and were supporting her as they made their way out the door.

Another had cut Cal's father free and helped him to his feet before leaning into the hallway, weapon at the ready.

They were really saved. Free. Just like that. It was amazing. Surreal.

"Fuck," Cal bit out.

"What's wrong?" she asked, knowing their uneventful escape was too good to be true.

His intense blue eyes framed by the mask locked onto hers. "We're about to have company."

CHAPTER TWENTY-SEVEN

"Vehicle inbound," Roxy announced into the earpiece in Cal's ears.

When he let out a cuss at that unfortunate information, Pru of course noticed and questioned him.

"We're about to have company." Grabbing her arm, he almost dragged her toward the door. "Follow Vito out. I'll be right behind you."

He gave her a little shove, sending her into the hall behind Vito who, equipped with a similar earpiece, had heard the bad news and knew they needed to move and fast, just as Vincent and Rocky did as they hustled his weakened grandmother toward the door after Pru.

Then there was his father who stood there looking as useless as he was. "What's happening?" he demanded in a tone that led Cal to think the man thought he was in charge. That couldn't be further from the truth.

"The men who kidnapped you are on their way inside. And if you don't want to be their guest any longer, I suggest you move." Cal resisted the urge to prod his father into action with the butt of his weapon, but it was a struggle. When his father still didn't move, he said, "Go! Move it!"

As he watched Vincent and Rocky, one each under Myra's arms to help get her down the flight of stairs at the end of the warehouse's grungy hallway, the similarities to his last mission, the one in Russia, hit him hard. He remembered the older woman being helped down the stairs. The younger one jogging down them toward freedom. The unfortunate hospital guard stumbling upon them...

They'd gotten into the warehouse with no trouble. Without encountering a soul. That had made him nervous. Where were the kidnappers? When would they be back? How many would there be when they returned? With the news of a vehicle inbound, it seemed one of those questions had been answered.

What he did know was they were amateurs. They'd left high value hostages alone. In a warehouse connected to their own corporation. Thank God they were bad at being bad guys because their ineptitude had led him, with Eva's help, right to his family. But they weren't in the clear yet.

"Second vehicle inbound," Roxy's voice announced into all their ears.

"Fuck, fuck, fuck!" Cal bit out again. They might have to shoot their way out of here. He trusted the guys—and his female sniper—to be able to handle themselves in a shootout, but there were three civilians to deal with. Three of his family members, which complicated things even more.

"Calvin. Language." Myra managed to look over her shoulder to reprimand him, to the great delight of the two mobsters laughing hysterically over her comment, despite their position getting worse by the minute.

Cal let out a huff. "Yes, ma'am. But we gotta move. We've got incoming."

"Yeah. I heard it. We're moving as fast as we can," Rocky turned back to snap.

Vito was up ahead on point, taking the lead and clearing the way down the stairs to the basement exit which led to the back of the building where they'd parked the vehicles. Pru was right behind Vito and although it was killing Cal to not have her tucked safely beside him, he had to trust his team. And even if Vito could be an ass in the barber shop, he was turning out to be a good team member when the chips were down.

Hopefully whoever was arriving would come in by the main entrance at the front of the building on the first floor.

Cal was bringing up the rear, making sure if there was somebody who was going to pursue them, they didn't get far. With him was his father, who seemed to move slower than his grandmother although he didn't look at all injured.

Shouting and the sound of booted feet pounding on the floor above proceeded the stairwell door banging open. They'd discovered the hostages were gone and were no doubt searching for them. At least one had chosen to take the basement stairs, just as they had, and was in pursuit.

Cal saw the gun first, held out in one hand as the guy grabbed the handrail with his other. He was more focused on not falling down the stairs as he rounded the landing, weapon up. The man was in his sights by the time he even saw Cal blocking the stairway, shielding his father behind him.

He was falling from Cal's double shot, one to his chest and one to his head, before he had a chance to squeeze off even a single round. It looked like he was alone, but that might not be the case for long. The sound of discharging the weapon was deafening in the stairwell. The dead guy's friends would have heard it. They could be on their way there now.

Cal spun, and almost crashed into the frozen form of his father. The old man, pale with a glistening sheen of sweat on his forehead, wasn't handling watching his son kill a man very well. They didn't have time for a therapy session or for Cal to explain it had been an *us or them situation.* He couldn't tell his father this was work and at that moment the man was not a person, but a target. A threat. Something that needed to be eliminated.

All he did say was, "Dad! Keep moving."

That knocked his father out of his stupor. He turned, lost his footing in his leather bottomed dress shoes and slid down one step. But he managed to grab the handrail, righted himself and scrambled down the remainder of the stairs.

"How's it looking outside?" Cal asked as Vito eased open the door, weapon first.

"Clear exit. Back of the building is clear," Roxy reported.

As Vito grabbed Pru's arm and pulled her outside and to where they'd left the vehicles by the door against the back of the building, Cal truly hoped the coast was clear, because Vito had hold of the woman Cal had plans for. He wasn't going to lose her now.

Cal got his father outside and, using both hands and all his might, shoved the dumpster next to the back door a few feet over so it was blocking the exit door from opening.

He saw his father get into the passenger side of the Bronco. After making sure Pru and his grandmother had been hustled safely into Vincent's oversized SUV, Cal jumped into the driver's seat.

Banging and lots of shouting told him the dumpster had done its job, but he wasn't going to wait around to see for how long. Tires screeched as he peeled out backwards, shifted to drive and sped out of the parking lot.

He saw Roxy climbing down from her sniper hide, the platform of a billboard along the road just past the warehouse's driveway.

"I got Roxy," he said into the com unit as he swerved the Bronco onto the shoulder and waited for her to sprint to him.

"Thanks, kid. I got Myra and your girl. Meet you back at the mansion," Vincent said, proving Cal wasn't fooling anyone by calling Pru *his cousin*. And that there was no denying his family was rich as hell and did indeed live in a freaking mansion. But none of that seemed to matter to Vincent, so Cal wasn't going to worry about it.

Roxy crawled into the back seat behind him. As he floored it, sending road dirt shooting out from behind the Bronco, she leaned forward between the seat, beaming.

"Woo! That was a hell of a good time. Two went in. How many did you take out inside?" she asked.

"One," Cal answered.

She nodded before she spun to watch out the back. "Oops. Looks like it's not over yet. Vehicle in pursuit. No worries. I got you, bro."

One glance in the rearview mirror told Cal Roxy was right. There was a vehicle hot on their heels. The sound of two shots being fired had him glancing in the mirror again to see she had successfully taken out the car's front tires, sending it careening to the shoulder.

"Looks like we're in the clear now," she said, while laying the sniper rifle across her lap and leaning back, her arms stretched out wide along the back seat.

Cal's father, eyes wide and skin still lacking any color shook his head. "Who the hell are these people?"

"They're my team," Cal told him as he yanked off

the black ski mask and tossed it between them in the console. "And my friends."

"Hell, yeah. Battle buddies for life," Roxy said, grinning at him in the mirror.

Cal couldn't help but smile at the truth of what she said.

CHAPTER TWENTY-EIGHT

P ru had begun to piece together who Cal's team was by the time they'd reached the turnoff for the house. They were not SEALs. The Apalachin mob seemed more likely. Vincent tenderly tending to Myra the whole way home was one big clue. Cal had told her he thought there was history between them, as odd as that seemed.

As Vito drove, Rocky played host and gave her his own bottle of water to share with Myra. He apologized they hadn't thought to bring more. That they'd been in a hurry and didn't think it was smart to stop along the way to buy supplies.

That was fine with her. She wouldn't feel truly safe until she was upstairs on the third floor in her own bedroom, possibly with her dresser pushed in front of her locked door.

She'd never wander around the first floor of the house at night alone again. She'd never look out the big windows on the first floor at the beautiful landscaping again either without remembering how someone had taken advantage of all that glass to break in.

It was going to take a long time to recover from this and her dehydration was the least of it. But as the house came into view, it seemed like they'd actually gotten away. She was safe. It would take time but, against all odds, things would be normal again.

That thought propelled her from the parked SUV, up the front stairs and right up to the front door. Which was locked. And since she was in last night's oversized T-shirt and shorts, she had no key.

She knocked and rang the bell. All she wanted was to go inside, chug a gallon of water, eat if her fluttering stomach would allow that, and shower. She couldn't shake the dirty feel of being captive in the warehouse from her skin. Or from her soul.

"What the hell?" Vincent said behind her.

"Did we just drive into a fucking ambush?" Vito asked.

She turned to glance at Vincent, then up at the

second floor where his gaze was pinned. Directly above her there was a shotgun sticking out of the window, aimed right at the men in the drive.

Myra still stood in the drive by the vehicle. From there she must have had a better view of who wielded the weapon because she said, "Good God, Agnes, put that thing away before you shoot someone."

"That's the whole idea of a gun, Myra. You okay?"

"Yes, I'm okay. Don't I look okay?" Myra asked, sounding insulted.

"Honestly, you've looked better. These guys holding you hostage?" Agnes asked.

"No. They're the ones who rescued me. Along with Cal. Open the damn door. I need to sit down."

The door flung wide and Cadence came running out, Myra's friend Linda on her heels.

Cadence looked hysterical as she rushed to hug first Pru then Myra. Linda looked confident and happy. "I told them you were okay now, but they didn't believe me."

Given how often Linda was right, they'd better all start believing her.

"Hell of a group of friends you got here, Myra," Vincent commented, finally taking his focus off the balcony now that Agnes had lowered her weapon and gone inside.

"Aren't they?" She beamed.

The arrival of Cal, with Senior and a much too attractive young woman who seemed to be related somehow to the other guys, caused more chaos.

Inside the cross talking and animated conversations by those who'd been home waiting and those who'd been in the heart of the action had Pru's head aching. She slipped away to the powder room to take care of business and get an aspirin.

When she opened the door, Cal was there, concern in his expression. "You all right?"

"Yes. Just a headache."

"Drink more."

"I will."

He ran his hands up her arms and pulled her close. "I was so scared."

She leaned into him, resting her forehead on his chest. "That makes two of us."

He pulled back. "I gotta deal with these guys, but after—"

"After?"

He tipped his head to the side. "I don't intend on leaving your side."

"Okay." She smiled.

Back in the living room, where Senior had been uncharacteristically quiet as he drank heavily from the decanter at his side, Cal stood and tried to get the attention of the unruly group.

"We're going to need to call the police," he said.

That was met with grumbles from his crew.

"Shoulda never called them to begin with," Rocky mumbled.

"Amateurs," Vito added.

"We need to get your stories straight. They're going to ask questions and you need to have good answers. Why were you there? How did you find the warehouse?" Vincent began.

"How did that guy end up ventilated with two holes in him in the stairwell?" Rocky finished.

"All good questions the police would probably want answers to." Roxy, who had made Pru irrationally jealous by arriving with Cal, nodded.

"How *did* you find the warehouse?" Cadence asked.

Cal had forgotten he hadn't filled her in on all the details.

"A hacker friend of Cal's," Rocky supplied, making it sound worse than it really was.

"You know a hacker? Who? Where did you meet them?" Cadence demanded.

Cal jumped to explain. "I don't know her. We never met. She lives in Bitter End, Tennessee. I got her name from a guy I know."

Cadence's eyes narrowed. "Why is that name so familiar? Ooo, I know. There was a rumor that one of the sorority girls at Cornell moved there right after graduation. Poppy...Van Clief. That was her name. It was the talk of the campus that she'd shunned her family in the Hamptons to move to some town no one ever heard of. What a coincidence, right?"

"Can we get back to the problem at hand?" Myra prompted. "What are we supposed to tell the police when they interview us?"

"I'll say I went in alone," Cal offered. "We won't involve you guys at all."

"That's fine, but where's the gun you used? Where did you get it? Is that semi-automatic legally registered to you?" Rocky continued, listing more possible questions the authorities would ask. "That's what they're going to want to know. What are you going to answer?"

"I don't know. Let me think." Cal drew in a breath and ran one hand over his face in frustration.

"Do you have to tell them anything? Can't we just say the ladies came home on their own?" Vito suggested.

Cal shook his head. "There's still at least one guy out there, possibly more, who could come back here and try to finish the job."

"Besides that, my group and I are going to expose this sham of a charity selling Narcan instead of giving it away. I don't care what you say, we have to report them. They're not getting away with that," Myra pronounced.

Her friend Sue from the charity nodded next to her. "I agree. We have to."

"You always were a little spitfire." Vincent's brown eyes softened as he gazed at Myra and crinkled in the corners from his smile.

"We could make up a story. Pretend the crew who took them fought among themselves. One shot the other and you took the opportunity to escape. But there are three of you. The cops are gonna separate you to take statements and if the stories don't match…" Rocky let the sentence trail off so they could all fill in their own idea of what the consequences might be.

None of the scenarios Pru could come up with were good.

"Okay. I got it. This is what we're going to do…" Cal began and the people in the room actually quieted to listen.

They were probably as interested in what idea he'd come up with as she was, because right now, she didn't see any way out of this.

CHAPTER TWENTY-NINE

"So, you're telling me you had a hunch about the building where the hostages might be being held, checked it out and found not only your three family members, but also one of the alleged perpetrators, shot, dead. Is that right?"

"That's correct." Cal nodded.

"And how do you think that happened? Him being already shot like that," Officer Nolan, a tall, thin man who looked like he was counting the days until his retirement would kick in, asked.

Cal shrugged. "There's no way for me to tell for certain since it happened before I arrived, but I'd guess there was dissent between the kidnappers. It's not too hard to imagine a disagreement turning violent with the sort of people who would break in and take an old woman from her home in the middle of the night."

"Mm-hm." The officer made notes and then looked up. "And the only three witnesses to all this, your family members, can't corroborate your story because they were knocked out when you found them?"

"Yes, sir." Luckily the handkerchief they'd used to sedate his father had been still hanging around the old man's neck.

Cal had supplied that to the officer upon his arrival. It provided the evidence for Cal's lie that all three were unconscious until he arrived. That he'd cut their ties loose and removed the gags, which roused them so they could make it down the stairs and to his Bronco.

Before she left, Roxy had confirmed she didn't see any cameras on the exterior of the building and he hadn't seen any on the inside. With no video evidence to the contrary, the police really had no other course of action except to believe Cal.

"And you decided to check that particular building because..." Nolan prompted.

Cal was prepared for this and had his answer set.

"In my ten years as a Navy SEAL I've been trained to analyze situations such as this. I determined that whoever had taken my family members wouldn't want to travel too far. They'd be too exposed in a vehicle. Since my father was taken from his factory in Albany and my grandmother and cousin from this house, on a map of the area I triangulated the locations of the two kidnappings with any abandoned buildings. I particularly looked for any off the beaten path, but still within a close proximity to both kidnapping sites. My plan was to start searching those closest then expand the search area as needed. Turns out, I got lucky and found them."

It was all bull shit and the cop looked torn between being pissed that the police department hadn't done the same and broken the case themselves, and doubtful that SEALs had such awesome training that Cal was able to perform such a miracle on his own.

"Yes. Very lucky." Scowling, the officer moved. "Now, Mr. Swenson—"

"Cal, please." He tried not to cringe at being addressed in a way he associated with his father, rather than himself.

"Cal, do you own any weapons?"

That question no doubt stemmed from the fact a squad car had already been dispatched to the warehouse and picked up the man Cal had dispatched with three rounds from the Thompson M1928.

Yes, they'd supplied him with an actual Tommy

Gun, just like in the old movies. Not a surprise, really. Vincent seemed the type to hold on to tradition.

But Cal wasn't about to mention *that* gun.

"Me personally? Yes. I have a Sig registered to me. It's back in Coronado. That's in California," he explained, being a smart ass while trying not to sound like one.

"Yes, I know where it is." The cop narrowed his eyes.

"The team weapons I use are not owned by me personally. My M1014 Joint Service Shotgun. My M4A1 carbine, for close quarters. You know, shorter barrel. Then there's the Mossberg 590. The Glock... All of those remain on base when we're not on missions or training. Along with the other equipment, like my NODS...uh, sorry. That stands for Night Observation Devices."

Cal's sheer volume of word vomit was designed to overwhelm the cop. And it looked like it was working. He no longer looked doubtful.

In fact, he looked a little envious of all Cal's toys. That was very good considering the amount of lies he'd told the authorities today.

But it looked like he was in the clear. That had been aided immensely by Myra's long time personal friend from the country club, a recently retired doctor who'd made an actual house call to check out her, Pru and his father.

With just a little prompting by Cal, the doctor was happy to strongly advise against any extended questioning given what the three had been through that day.

Actually, the hardest part had been getting Myra's friends to leave. Agnes, who he'd heard had apparently leveled a gun on the Apalachin crew until they proved they were friendlies, and Linda who was so much like Blessing it was eerie, and Sue the one who'd truly broken the case for him with her information about the vending machines, only left after multiple promises that Myra would keep in touch.

As it was, Agnes was only going as far as Linda's house, instead of heading back to Mudville right away. *Just in case*, the tough old lady had said.

Cadence had disappeared upstairs with Pru and her dog. His sister had no desire to speak with the police, which was a relief. She tended to babble at times. The staff were all sent home. It had been one hell of a day for them too. They deserved to go home early— and the fewer people to answer questions in this situation, the better.

The Apalachin crew hadn't had to be convinced to skedaddle before the authorities showed up, so that had been easy. Vincent had left with all the information Cal had gotten from Eva about ownership on the warehouse. And he'd promised to look into things with the vending machines and the shell company who'd gotten the grant for them.

Vincent had the resources to find anyone connected to the guy Cal had taken out, and to make sure they were scared enough to never try anything that foolish again.

Sadly, Cal had more faith in Vincent getting the job done than the cop who'd responded that morning who'd kept telling him his grandmother and Pru had probably just gone out shopping, *like rich ladies tend to do*."

"I guess I got all I need." Nolan flipped his notebook closed. "You gonna be around in case I have more questions?"

Cal nodded. "I'm scheduled to be here for a month, unless I get recalled."

"That happen a lot?" the officer asked.

Cal wobbled his head. "It happens."

He fought the urge to knock wood to insure it didn't happen this time. For once he wasn't all that anxious to leave here.

"All right. Have a good night."

"Thanks. You too, officer." Cal closed and locked the door behind the man and let out a breath. It felt as if he hadn't truly breathed since this morning when he'd found Pru's cell phone and pieced together what had happened.

His father crept out of his study at the sound of the front door closing. "They buy your story?"

"It seems so. Thank God." He raised his gaze to his father and noticed his color hadn't quite returned. "You all right?"

"Just a headache from whatever they knocked me out with, but otherwise..." The old man shrugged.

Cal had literally saved his dad's life. He been hoping that perhaps the man might show him and his chosen profession a little bit more respect now. That was probably a lot to ask of someone so chronically self-centered.

"I wanted to say thanks," his father said, not making eye contact.

Wonders never ceased. An actual thanks, although delivered begrudgingly.

But for once, Cal didn't want thanks, or even respect. What he wanted wasn't for himself.

He leveled his gaze on his father. "I don't want your gratitude. But there is something I want you to do."

"What's that?" He looked suspicious.

"I want you to give Pru the money that's in her trust fund now instead of making her wait for it."

He shook his head. "I can't. It's locked down."

"Aren't you the executor? Can't you choose to turn it over early?" Cal asked.

His father shook his head. "She's just a kid. She'll blow it on something stupid."

"She's been more adult than any of us since the week she turned eighteen and became an orphan. What if she wants to go back to school? Move out. Get her own place and a job that doesn't entail being Grandmother's go-for."

"Your assumption is wrong—" His father held up one hand to block Cal's protest. "About the executorship. It's not me. It's the lawyer who drew up the will."

"So, make good on the money now out of your own account. It was shortsighted of Uncle Guy to think he was invincible. That he'd be around until he was old and gray and died a natural death long after Pru had a college education. Or a new car. Or the wedding of her dreams or whatever else she might want. He'd want her to have what she needs. What she wants."

"And her waiting two years will make that big of a difference?" his old man asked.

Cal thought back to Pru, waiting on his grandmother like she was one of the house staff. Always thinking of Myra first before herself. Not because she loved the old woman and wanted to do it, which he was sure she did, but because she was obligated to. For her room and board and whatever pittance they paid her. Out of fear of losing the only security she had left.

He nodded. "Yeah, Dad. I think it will make all the difference in the world. And after today, she deserves it. Deserves to have the means to leave if she wants to."

His father's pinched mouth didn't bode well for a positive outcome, but finally, he nodded. "Okay. I'll have money transferred into an account for her."

"The full amount?" Cal asked.

It looked like it pained him, but he nodded. "The full amount."

"Good. Thank you. Now I'm going upstairs. It's been one hell of a day." Cal suddenly had an overwhelming urge to check on Pru.

More than check on her.

He needed to hold her. Feel her body, warm, alive and safe beneath his. Now that the adrenaline was gone, and his job was done, the full scope of the horrific situation she'd been in hit him hard.

He strode toward the staircase but as he went, he heard a sound come out of his father he rarely heard. An actual laugh before the old man said, "Helluva day. Ha. You're not kidding."

CHAPTER THIRTY

After letting the hot water pound away the tension and wash away the stink of fear and the memories of the warehouse, Pru emerged from the shower feeling worlds better.

She exchanged the towel for a fresh oversized T-shirt and was about to find a pair of shorts or yoga pants to pull on when a hard knock sounded on her door.

Her heart thundered. Cadence had just left her after finally believing she was fine and that the only thing she desperately needed was a shower.

Unless someone had sent a member of the staff up with something for her, that left one person who could be at her door. Cal.

"Come in."

The door swung in and a determined Cal strode inside. As her pulse raced, he only paused long enough to close and lock the door before he continued his path directly to her.

Her feet left the floor as he hauled her up against him. His mouth found hers and he wasted no time claiming it with his tongue.

She ended up perched on top of the low dresser in her room with Cal standing between her spread thighs as he kissed her breathless. It wrenched a sound of pleasure from her that broke whatever self-control they both had left.

This—him with her like this—was everything she'd ever dreamed.

She reached between them, tugging on the button at his waist while he shoved the bottom of her T-shirt up, over her hips and higher until his palms bracketed her ribcage and his thumbs brushed her breasts.

"I thought I'd lost you," he gasped between kisses.

"You didn't," she said, still working on getting him naked by easing down the zipper on his cargo shorts.

"I almost went out of my mind," he confessed.

That was followed by a groan as she wrapped her hand around his hard length.

"Stop or I won't be able to control myself," he warned but made no move to step away or stop her.

He could wrestle with his own conscience and misplaced sense of honor if he wanted, but she took his lack of movement as a sign to proceed.

"I don't want you to control yourself." She gave him another stroke and felt the last thread of his resolve disappear.

It was as if something snapped inside him. He sucked in a breath as he lifted her and spun toward the bed.

She hit the mattress, but he didn't follow her down. He stepped back, but only long enough to kick off his shoes and shorts.

As he stalked toward her on the bed, he pulled his shirt off over his head and tossed it to the floor then stepped out of his underwear—bright red boxer briefs.

Cal was breathtaking on a regular day. But naked and crawling onto the bed to brace over her, he was magnificent. And she wasn't letting him get away. Not this time.

Pru reached down to tug off her own shirt. She tossed it and then reached for the drawer in the side table. She pulled out a small box of condoms. She wanted no reason, no excuse, for them to not finish this tonight.

His gaze hit on what was in her hand. She prepared for his protest. For him to tell her they were taking things slow. But it didn't come. Instead a look of relief crossed his face.

"Thank God," he said on a breath as he reached for the box, tore into the cardboard then broke into one of the packets.

Then latex was the only thing between them as he lowered his body over hers. Impatient, she grasped the firm globes of his ass in both hands and tugged him closer.

He groaned again but resisted her efforts. "You're not ready," he gasped.

"I've been ready for five years," she countered.

That elicited another groan on his part as his mouth covered hers again. Cal slipped his hand between them. He slid his fingers expertly over her slick folds and moaned, "You're so wet."

"Told you I'm ready."

This time he didn't argue with her. Didn't fight. Didn't make excuses. He lined up the blunt tip of his length with her entrance and, gaze never leaving hers, slid inside.

She gasped as he filled her. So big. So hard. She glanced down, expecting to see him all the way in, but what she saw was only an inch or two inside her.

"So damn tight." A frown creased Cal's brow above his closed eyes as he held still. Then those blue eyes opened and he glanced down between them to where he was barely inside. "You're not ready."

"I am," she protested.

"No, you're not." He pulled back and she prepared to argue more. But he didn't get up. Didn't try to leave her.

Instead he slid down her body and latched his mouth onto her core as he thrust two, then three fingers inside her.

As he worked her with his hand and mouth she anticipated a repeat of their first time together, when he'd done this then left, and protested, "Cal, I want you inside me."

"Patience, Pru" was all he said before attacking her with his teeth, then soothing her with the flat of his tongue.

When he pulled on her tender flesh, sucking her hard while stroking a spot deep inside, her hips lifted of their own accord.

That encouraged Cal to double down on his efforts until the building wave of pleasure crested, crashing over her.

He slapped one hand over her mouth as she let out a loud cry that filled the room, but he continued to push her higher.

Her muscles clenched and spasmed and Cal

reacted. His movements became more frenzied until he broke away and landed on top of her.

Hooking his hand beneath one of her bent knees, he lifted her leg high and thrust inside her with one firm stroke. Her body was still quivering with spasms as he pressed all the way inside this time and held deep.

His back bowed with that first thrust, which he repeated, again and again. Slowly at first, but then quickening with an increasing tempo until Cal pressed and held deep, let out a moan and emptied himself into the condom while buried inside her.

It was so much more than her inexperienced teenaged self in the past had imagined being with Cal would be like. Even her adult self was in awe.

"Can we talk about the box of condoms?" Cal asked, his voice muffled as he still lay on top of her with his face partially buried in her pillow.

"What about it?" she asked, feigning innocence.

He finally moved, making him slip out of her as he lay on his side and propped up on one elbow to pin her with his gaze. "Is this something you routinely keep stocked in your bedroom drawer?"

She heard the shadow of jealousy in the question and loved it.

Her lips twitched and she briefly toyed with the

idea of teasing him, but she couldn't do it. She wanted no doubt in Cal's mind that she was all his. That determined that she had to tell him the truth.

"Your sister gave those to me as a gag gift for my twenty-first birthday."

At the time, Cadence had said it was because Pru needed to stop working so hard at school and her part time job and get laid already.

"Two years ago," Cal repeated. A smile tugged at the corners of his lips. "You never opened the box."

She had a feeling they weren't really talking about her not opening the box, but something else entirely. He was asking if he was her first.

"I never opened the box," she confirmed, answering his unspoken question. Maybe she'd been saving herself for him. Or maybe no real boy or man could live up to her lifelong fantasies of Calvin Swenson Junior.

The answer earned her a look from Cal that would live in her memory for the rest of her life. Possessive. Satisfied. Masculine. Intense.

He hauled her close and claimed her mouth one more time. And that's not all he claimed again. They used one more of those condoms before he was done and they lay, damp with sweat and sated on her bed.

When both of their breathing had finally returned

to normal, Cal said lazily, "That's a lot of books you got there."

She glanced at the piles on top of the dresser. The stacks looked a little more precarious after the recent amorous activity that had taken place on the dresser where they were. A lot less neat now than they'd been before Cal's arrival. In fact, one pile looked a lot like the Leaning Tower of Pisa.

"I like books," she said simply, figuring no further explanation was needed.

"You might have noticed that this house does have a few bookshelves. Like all over," he pointed out.

Shelves all over, except in her room.

She left that fact unspoken and said, "Yes. And I've read a lot of what's on those shelves. And what I haven't read is—I hate to say this—pretty unreadable. Like reference books about nineteenth and twentieth century farming and industrial equipment and stuff like that."

"Yeah. I noticed that myself. But what I was suggesting was that you could add your books to the collection," he said with perfect sincerity.

She let out a snort of a laugh. "Yeah. No. I can't see your father allowing any of *my* books on his shelves."

"Why not?"

If Cal really had to ask that, he'd been away from

home for too long. He must have forgotten what a horrible man his father was. Good for him. But she couldn't forget.

Besides the fact that the books were Pru's, and she was not really a member of the family in Senior's opinion, she had other very good reasons. "Because most of mine are mostly paperbacks, and not antiques and leather bound with gilded edges. And they're romance novels. And some of them are pretty... *spicy.*"

Cal pulled back to deliver a surprised glance in her direction. "Oh are they? How *spicy?*" he asked with a smile.

"Stop looking so intrigued." She scowled, picturing what he must be imagining.

"Why? It's intriguing."

She smiled at his continued interest in what was between the pages of her books but didn't comment.

"Cadence has nice shelves in her room," he pointed out unnecessarily, leaning his head on his hand.

Pru sighed. "Yes, she does."

"I don't think she has any books on them. Last I looked it was all...stuff," he continued.

"Yes, it is." Shelf upon beautiful shelf, scattered with stuff. And not one book among it all, if she didn't count the school yearbooks.

"Hey, why don't you read me some of your books? Maybe the spicy parts." He waggled his eyebrows.

"Cal! No. I couldn't," she squealed.

"Then how about we act it out instead?" He grabbed her around the waist and rolled them so she was on top, straddling him naked beneath her.

"I'll consider it," she said before leaning low and kissing him into silence.

CHAPTER THIRTY-ONE

To say he was in a good mood was an understatement.

Cal hadn't felt this good in forever. But it wasn't just the sex…and there had been lots of that. Or even today's successful mission that had returned his family to him safely. It was Pru who had him walking around the house feeling like his feet were barely touching the ground.

She was quick and smart. Beautiful but modest. Genuine and caring. But also insecure. And if he had to make love to her all night every night for the month he was home just to knock that hesitant uncertain look out of her eyes, he was willing to do that.

Not that it would be a hardship on him. She was passionate and sexy. And she was his, which seemed to expose a caveman-like possessive side he hadn't realized he had. It had never shown itself with any woman before. Not that he'd gotten all that close with anyone.

The Navy was the longest and most serious relationship in his life and had been since he'd turned eighteen. Being with Pru was the first time he'd seriously considered changing that.

Maybe it shouldn't be a surprise they would eventually be together. That they'd fit so perfectly. They'd both experienced dramatic life changes very young. Her when her mom had married Guy. Him when he'd lost his mother. Then again at eighteen. Him when he chose the Navy. Her when circumstances took her parents.

The inevitability of it all had him smiling as he opened the door to his bedroom. He'd finally left Pru alone to get some sleep. As much as he'd wanted to stay, she needed the rest after the day she'd had. And he needed to be far enough away from her he wasn't tempted to keep waking her up for yet another round.

Inside his bathroom, he stripped and showered, resisting the temptation to give himself a tug when memories of Pru had him getting semi hard in the shower stall. Clean and satisfied, he was still walking on air as he towel-dried his hair... until his cell phone lit on the dresser.

He could hope it was Pru, sending him a text saying she missed him or something sweet. Or his sister forwarding a silly meme or TikTok. But a twisting in his gut, some sixth sense, told him it wasn't either of those things.

This time of night, and given he'd just left Pru and that his sister was probably in bed, it had to be something else.

West Coast.

The words crossed his mind, bringing with them a sense of dread. It wasn't late there.

Please let it be one of the team checking in.

He reached for the cell and opened the text. It was one of the team, all right, but it wasn't a simple check-in. It was Slim, telling him he might want to get back to Coronado sooner rather than later or it might be *too late*.

The message was vague but he knew Slim well enough and had been in the teams long enough he could read between the lines. The team must have been put on call to be spun up for some mission Slim knew Cal would want to be on. And it could be leaving soon. Long before his leave was up and he returned home.

He dialed his Lieutenant Commander. Even at six p.m. California time the O-4 was on duty and answered his cell phone on the first ring.

"Swenson. I had a feeling I might be hearing from you. How are things at home?"

"Good, sir. Better. I could come back—if you needed me."

Smyth barked out a laugh. "Who messaged you?"

"Um—"

"It's all right. I'm assuming you don't know details."

"Yes, sir. That's correct."

"And you want them."

What could he say? Yes, he wanted them. So badly. But this wasn't a secure line and he wasn't going to get them. But he hoped the LT would give him something. Anything.

"How quickly can you get back here?" Smyth continued.

"I'll have to check flights. Maybe I can get on a late one tonight. Or first thing tomorrow morning."

"I want you to know, we can do this without you. I've got coverage if you're still needed at home."

Was he needed? His grandmother and Pru were safe.

He had told the cop he'd be around in case they had more questions, but military orders trumped that.

There was still the problem of the guy who'd gotten away. And possible retaliation over the one he'd taken out. He didn't know how deep this thing went.

The threat hadn't been completely eliminated and he hated leaving before it was.

"Can I get back to you on that?" Cal asked.

"Yes. Just don't wait too long or it'll be a moot point," the senior commissioned officer warned.

He wanted to ask how long was too long but knew he wouldn't get an answer on that while he was on a personal cell phone. It was tempting to drive to the nearest damn military base and ask to use a secure line and find out what the hell was going on.

Stewart in Newburgh wasn't all that far. But the National Guard there would think he was a lunatic driving in and asking to use the phone.

He'd have to make this decision blind. But he needed more information about the situation here at home to do that. And he knew where to go to get it.

"Understood. Thank you, sir. I'll get back to you." Cal disconnected the call and immediately made another one.

When the ringing stopped, he heard, "Hello."

"Vincent. I have a problem."

"Another one?" The man laughed.

"No. The same one. But now the problem is me. I need to go."

"When?"

"Now."

"And you're worried about your family and the loose ends."

"Exactly."

"We've got you covered, boy. You have my word. Nothing with happen to your family."

"Thank you."

Vincent let out another short laugh. "You'll pay me back. One day."

Cal had a feeling he might have just sold his soul to the mob but if it kept Pru and his grandmother, and Cadence and even his father safe, it was something he was willing to do. "Yes, I will."

He disconnected then typed in a text to his commander saying he'd let him know what flight he got on. As Cal hit send, he realized all that had been the easy part. The hard part was still ahead—telling Pru.

He walked up the stairs to her room with far less enthusiasm than he had a couple of hours ago. He hated to do it—didn't want to wake her if she was sleeping—but he had no choice. He knocked softly on her door then pushed it open. "Pru?"

She sat up on one elbow. "I was hoping you'd come back."

She sounded so happy. So hopeful. What he was about to say was going to destroy all of that.

Best to do it fast. Like ripping off a bandage. No words would make what he was about to say better. "I have to go back to California early."

"When?" The question was breathy and soft, as if she couldn't get enough air in her lungs to speak more loudly.

"Tonight."

Her eyes widened. "Oh."

"I didn't want to leave without saying goodbye."

She got up and wrapped her arms around his waist. He felt her shaking and it almost made him say fuck it and stay. But he didn't. He forced himself to pull away.

"I should go. I have to call a car to the airport and I've gotta try to get a flight."

"No, you will not call a car. I'm driving you to the airport. Well, it'll be in your Bronco but I can drive so you can work on getting a flight on your phone from the road."

She wanted to spend every last moment with him and he with her. But it had been a pretty horrible day and she had yet to sleep.

"Aren't you too tired?" he asked.

"No." She moved to the dresser and opened a drawer, pulling out a pair of stretchy pants. "I'm not going to be able to sleep knowing you're leaving anyway," she said, the pain obvious in her voice.

Pru opened a door and flipped on the light inside one of the neatest closets he'd ever seen. She tugged a sweatshirt off its hanger before she turned back, her face set, her expression serious, determined.

He reached out and stopped her frenzied effort to get dressed, turning her to face him.

"I'm so sorry I can't stay."

She was putting on a brave face, and he respected her for it, but he could see she was shaken over him leaving so suddenly. He pulled her closer and pressed a much too short kiss to her lips. Any longer and he'd be tempted to call the LT back and say he wasn't coming.

He pulled back and said, "I'll call and I'll text whenever I have a chance. I promise."

"You'd better," she said, eyes narrowed as she tried to act tough.

He smiled at her vehemence. "I will. And yeah, it would be nice to ride with you to the airport. Thanks."

There was only one more thing left to do. Get himself on a flight to San Diego.

No. Actually, there was another thing he wanted to do. Needed to do before he ended up God only knew where or for how long on the still undisclosed mission. And he needed to get it done while Pru wasn't in the Bronco with him.

There was a third thing that he tried not to think about too much because it was going to be the hardest of all. Saying goodbye to Pru when she dropped him off.

CHAPTER THIRTY-TWO

S omeone should research how one human body
could produce so much snot and so many tears.

Pru tossed yet one more saturated tissue at the
garbage pail in her bedroom. It landed heavily atop all
the rest. She was eleven for twelve in making it into
the pail. By the time she was finished crying over Cal
leaving she'd be ready for the NBA.

She'd feigned being tired from the kidnapping and
hid upstairs rather than going down to breakfast. No
one questioned her. The reality was, she would have
bounced downstairs, eaten breakfast and been ready
for an amazing day—if Cal wasn't halfway to
California by now.

Her eyes were too swollen and her nose too red to
show her face to the family. And there is no way she'd

be able to hear mention of Cal's sudden departure without tearing up. Or breaking down.

She sighed. This would pass. It had to. Eventually…

The sharp pain would turn to a dull ache. The twisting in her stomach and tight clenching of her heart would lessen. She'd go from feeling panic and pain to just having an ever-present shadow of discomfort.

She knew all that for a fact. That was how it had been after her mother and stepfather had died.

Heartbreak was just another form of grief, after all.

Her cell phone chimed with a text message and she scrambled to find it amid the tangled bedding. Cal's name on a new text message alert reminded her of one thing. Unlike her mother and stepfather, Cal wasn't dead. He was just gone. That added more layers to her grief. Hope. Fear. Doubt.

Holding on to all of the emotions, she tapped the alert to open the message.

Cal: Just landed. Will call when able. Keep a look out for a surprise today.

Hands shaking, she opened the window to reply, then considered what to say.

That she loved him. With her whole heart. So much she felt sick with it. That she was painfully sore in all the right places and hope that feeling never went away because it reminded her of him and what they did together.

The tears blurred the screen as she typed her reply.

Pru: Glad you arrived safely (Smiley face emoji) Will keep an eye out (Eyes emoji)

An hour later she heard a truck pull up to the front door. Heard men's voices she didn't recognize. She stumbled out of bed and to the window and saw the delivery truck. Then saw the two men open the rear and emerge with—a bookcase.

Cal. Her surprise. Memories of their discussion about books and shelves hit her. She unlocked her phone, her fingers flying over the keyboard.

Pru: Did you buy me a bookcase?!

Cal: Good. It's there. Enjoy. About to walk into a meeting. Talk later.

Maybe this long-distance thing could work. They'd text. They'd talk. He'd send gifts. She'd try her hand at sexting…

Her plans for how to survive this separation were cut short when she realized she looked like hell and was still in the T-shirt she'd slept in—with no bra.

Scrambling, she was very happy her room was on the third floor and there was no elevator. It gave her the time she needed to get herself together. She pulled on a sports bra and a T-shirt that actually fit and then grabbed the leggings she'd wore the night before to the airport. Then she realized she needed to clean the room.

She gathered the random clothes draped on the chair and dropped on the carpet and tossed them all onto the closet floor. She tugged up the sheet and comforter and straightened the pillows in a messy attempt to make the bed.

With a bit more time, judging by the sounds of bumping and grumbling from the second-floor staircase, she ran to the bathroom and splashed cold water on her face. A little cover-up beneath her eyes didn't negate the red rims, but at least it didn't look quite so much like she hadn't slept.

As ready as she was going to be, she headed for the back staircase just in time to meet Cadence coming up them. "Why didn't you tell me you were shopping for a bookcase for your room?"

Pru couldn't control her smile as she said, "I didn't buy it. Cal did. As a surprise."

Cadence's blonde brows rose as a smug smile twisted her lips. "I knew it. You two are perfect for each other."

Pru desperately wanted to believe her friend. And when two red faced men appeared at the bottom of the narrow staircase and gazed up at her with the heavy-looking white bookcase complete with gorgeous moldings that matched the style of the house braced between them she was actually inclined to believe it.

Less than an hour later, the bookcase was lagged safely to the wall in Pru's bedroom. The dresser had had to move, but she didn't mind it being inside her walk-in closet. Not at all.

She'd happily rearrange the closet to accommodate the piece of furniture if it meant she could have her dream bookcase in her bedroom.

After the men had been well tipped and had driven happily away, Pru and Cadence stood in front of the new piece.

"Now you have to fill it," Cadence observed.

Pru glanced at the piles of books that had been moved to the floor under the window when the dresser got taken out. "Not a problem."

She didn't mention there were more books under the bed. Cadence would see them soon enough.

After a rousing debate about how to arrange the shelves—by spine color or alphabetical by author— they started to sort and organize the books. Pru had nixed Cadence's idea to put them all spine in and pages out so it would present a *uniform color story*.

That was a hard no. Pru loved her books too much

to hide the titles. She wanted to see them in all their mismatched glory. But they did decide to organize the standalone titles by color, with a separate shelf dedicated to series that would be kept together in reading order.

And so as music to sort by pumped out of Cadence's phone the work began. Although something as fun could never be called work.

"What's this?" Cadence asked, about half an hour later.

Pru glanced up to see Cadence flipping through the sketchbook Pru hadn't seen, let alone touched, for years. But back then, she'd carry it around everywhere, filling it with pictures she'd drawn. Of the grounds. The family—mostly Cal. No surprise. And of her mom and her stepfather. Myra. Cadence. She'd even sketched the family's old, long gone, dog.

She remembered how Swanny, the Swenson's Brittany Spaniel, had been asleep in the sun on the porch and made the perfect subject.

But yeah, the pictures were mostly of Cal.

She used to love to draw. She'd stopped doing it completely the year her mother died.

Pru reached out and took the book from Cadence. "That's just my old sketch book. It's nothing. It doesn't belong on the bookcase."

"Those pictures are really good, Pru. You're really good. You should frame some and sell them online."

Pru frowned. "What? No." She shook her head.

"Then what do you want to do?" Cadence asked. "You're not going to be Myra's assistant forever. So what do you really want to be?"

It was something she'd let herself consider occasionally, until the fear shut down all thoughts of change and she scampered back to the comfort of the status quo.

"If you could do anything, anything at all, money is no object, what would you do?" Cadence prompted.

"Oh, so we're playing fantasy games now. Okay. If that's the question, then I think I'd want to go back to school."

"For what? Art?" Cadence suggested.

"No. That's more of a hobby. Fun. Not something I'd want to turn into a job. I don't know. Education, maybe. Or…" She let the silly thought trail off.

"Or?" Cadence encouraged.

Pru shook her head. "You're going to laugh."

"I won't. I promise." Cadence crossed her heart with one perfectly manicured finger. Pru curled her own fingers into her palm. She'd lost a considerable amount of nail polish and the tip of one nail trying to tear off the plastic ties at the warehouse.

Forget that.

"Library science," she said, forcing away the bad memory and getting back to Cadence's game.

"Library science." Her friend frowned until her eyes widened and she smiled. "You want to be a librarian?"

"Told you that you would laugh." Pru pouted.

"I'm not laughing at the idea. I'm laughing because it's so perfect for you. I couldn't have come up with something better. I mean, just look at us. Look at what we're doing. We're literally creating your own library for you here."

Pru couldn't deny the truth of that and what they were doing, even if her bookcase was tiny in comparison to the acre of shelves in the family's living room.

But the bookcase was from Cal, and she loved it. And she loved every book being put on its shelves, as much as she loved him... and she had no idea when she'd see him again, in spite of his promise he'd call as soon as he could.

Cadence had her phone out as she said, "Look at that. The University of Southern California offers an MS in Library Science."

Pru cocked up a brow. "California?"

Where Cal was. Cadence was playing matchmaker.

"What's wrong with California?" Cadence went on. "The weather is gorgeous."

"And it's going to look like I'm stalking your brother if I suddenly enrolled in school there."

Cadence shook her head. "I don't think he'd have any problem with that. Trust me."

Had Cal talked to Cadence about them? That made her love him even more.

Pru glanced at the cost of tuition on the cell's screen and almost choked. It was more money than she'd ever had in her life.

"It doesn't matter anyway because I don't have the money and your father's not going to pay for more education for me after he already paid for four years at Albany."

Cadence waved away her concern. "Let me talk to my dad."

"No. Please don't. Cadie, please. Promise me," Pru begged.

She remembered Senior's glare. The harsh *what are you staring at* in the warehouse. She wanted nothing from that man. It was bad enough she had to live in his house for lack of any other options. Even if she asked to move to one of the other houses on the property, it would still belong to him. And he'd no doubt grumble that heating a separate house just for her would be stupid when she could live here.

Best to leave things as they were. Going back to school to get her master's degree to become a librarian was a silly pipe dream. Just talk. Nothing would come of it.

A nagging voice in the back of her head reminded her being with Cal had also been just a dream and that had come true. That voice was followed by another one reminding her he was now gone again and she had no idea when she'd see him.

A knock on the door curtailed both the conversation with Cadence and her thoughts.

Pru slammed the door on the voices making her head spin and opened it to her visitor… and almost fell down when she saw Senior standing there.

She didn't think he even knew where her room was. Let alone would ever venture up the servants' stairs to get to it.

"Uh, is something wrong?" she asked him, assuming the worst. "Is Myra all right?"

She didn't know if she could take any more bad news right now.

"She's fine. Nothing's wrong." His gaze cut to his daughter. "Cadence. Can we have the room?" he asked, as if this were a board room and he needed his employees to clear out.

Whatever her father wanted to discuss, it was obvious Cadence wasn't privy to it. She stood for a second, her eyes cutting between them before she finally came out of her shocked, open-mouthed stupor and nodded.

"Yeah. Sure." She moved to the door. After she was behind her father and he couldn't see her, she mouthed to Pru, "Text me."

When the door was closed and they were alone—which was so freaking weird—Senior handed her a piece of paper. "Here."

"What's this?" She frowned down at it, not understanding the page that had her name on the top, and a six-figure dollar amount on the bottom.

"It's your new bank account. I suggest you move the bulk of it into an investment account that will earn you a higher yield. That way you can draw off the interest and not touch the balance."

She looked up. "I don't understand."

"That's the money in the trust that Guy left you."

"I can't touch that until I'm twenty-five." And holy hell, she remembered it being like half the amount at the reading of the will. It must have been invested well. It had grown over the years. By a lot.

Senior nodded. "That's right. But I'm advancing you the full amount now. So you have it to spend on... whatever." He looked less than thrilled to be telling her that.

It was more than enough to cover the cost if she did do it. Go to California. Get her master's degree. Was it crazy? Was she? Or was it exactly what she should do? What she needed.

No. She wasn't going to be spontaneous about this. She'd think about it seriously. Weigh her options. Consider all angles. It would be smarter to do what he said. Keep the money invested and earning interest. And then, eventually, use it to get her own place. Myra wouldn't be around forever...

Still, she had options now. Something she never felt she had before.

She wanted to yell and dance around the room. Throw her arms around someone and jump up and down. Senior was not the hugging type, or even a very nice person, although she'd have to reevaluate that opinion of him now. But he did deserve her gratitude for what he'd done.

"Thank you," she said with every ounce of sincerity in her body.

He nodded. "You're welcome." He turned to go, then turned back. "I'm sorry about what happened.

You didn't sign up for something like that when you became part of this family."

Then he left and left her in shock.

She had money. A lot of it. Senior considered her part of the family. Absolutely everything had changed. Just like five years ago. But this time, unlike then, the changes were definitely for the better.

Her phone vibrated in her hand. Glancing down she saw the text from Cal saying he'd call within the hour. Her heart leapt at that good news as she anticipated hearing his voice and telling him her good news.

CHAPTER THIRTY-THREE

C al sat in the meeting room bracketed by his teammates and glanced at the clock on the wall. For possibly the first time since joining the teams, his mind wasn't completely focused on the mission. It was on how he wished Smyth would wrap things up so he could get to his cell phone.

He'd texted Pru that he'd call within the hour and that was just about an hour ago. He wanted to check in with his grandmother before they went wheels up. And he wanted to touch base with Vincent. Let the man know he'd be out of communications range for a while. Instead he was sitting there trying to focus on mission critical information that could save his life.

This was why he didn't have serious relationships. But the problem was, he really wanted one. With Pru.

He forced his attention back to the commander. Cal finally knew why he'd flown back and Slim was right, he was happy he did—home matters aside.

An investigation by Ukrainian prosecutors using the images of the Russian soldiers who'd committed the war crime of basically murdering unarmed civilians had yielded a name. The identity of the officer on the video shooting the two unarmed office workers in the back. They had a name. They had a location. And they were sending his team in to get him.

The territory where the target was located was in turmoil. It was a disputed region. A port formerly used by Ukraine but currently held by Russian forces. It would be easy enough for his team to access the city from the water, slip in and out, unnoticed amid the chaos with the war criminal in their possession.

Nikolay Sergeevich Sokovikov was being charged with "violation of the laws and customs of war" and "international murder." Cal's unit was going in as part of a UN force, to aid bringing the man to justice.

This was a loose end the US was happy to tie up. After seeing the video, Cal was glad to be a part of it. He just needed to focus on the mission and deal with his feelings about leaving home and Pru when he got back.

The scene from just hours ago filled his mind. Leaving her standing there in Albany at the airport, crying as she watched him pass through the security checkpoint. Seeing her wave as the tears streamed down her face before he turned the corner for his gate.

The teams were hardest on those left behind, but it was no easy thing for the SEAL doing the leaving either.

But was it worth not having the good times, just to avoid the bad times?

He flashed back to Pru in the garden with Myra. Her handing over her big fat folder of the research that had her so excited. Her crying out his name while she was coming beneath him. Her stacks and stacks of books and her obsessively neat closet.

"Wheels up in an hour," Smyth said, bringing Cal back to the present.

An hour didn't leave him much time. Then again, when it came to matters of the heart, there'd never be *enough time*.

CHAPTER THIRTY-FOUR

A week.

Seven days.

One hundred and seventy-two hours to be exact. She'd figured it out.

That was how long it had been since Pru had last heard from Cal.

Yes, he'd warned her that where he was going he wouldn't be able to call or text or even email. He'd also said that usually wasn't the case so she shouldn't worry. Ops like this, where they had no communications, happened infrequently. He'd be back before she knew it then they'd talk all the time.

They could even make plans for a visit. She could come to him if he couldn't get to her. He'd buy the ticket. She could stay at his place. Or they'd get a room at the hotel in Coronado, if she wanted.

Holding on tight to all his promises and googling the gorgeous Hotel del Coronado had kept Pru sane… for about three days.

Day four things started to get tougher. Day five it all seemed like a cosmic joke. Like the universe was keeping her from Cal and happiness on purpose.

By day six she started to question if it was all real. Had he meant it when he said he'd call? What if these days away had given him time to think, to reconsider them being together, and he'd changed his mind?

He could be there right now, sitting in Coronado with his phone turned off so her calls were going right to voicemail and her texts were showing as not delivered. Or worse, maybe he'd blocked her number until she got the hint or he figured out how to tell her he didn't want to be with her anymore.

On the morning of day seven she resigned herself to it being over with Cal.

She'd been moving through her days on auto pilot. Cadence had gone back to Ithaca and Senior back to work. It was easy to go through the motions with Myra. They had a schedule. A system. But suddenly, she didn't want to do it anymore. Couldn't face going back to the way things had been.

Getting out her computer, she opened a search window. The VPN icon in the corner of her screen reminded her of Cal. Everything reminded her of Cal. She needed to do something new, go somewhere new. Different. That wouldn't remind her of him.

Right after Senior had given her the money, she'd brought up possibly going back to school to Myra, just in case she did decide one day to actually do it, and Myra had been nothing but supportive. It helped the old lady seemed to be occupied with both her charity and a certain Apalachin mob boss.

If Pru was going to do this, now was the time.

She typed in Masters Degrees in Library Sciences and began her research.

The California program came up, of course. She forced herself to look at all the others and ignore that one until finally, it was one of the only ones left to look at. And of course California did look beautiful. And the campus was incredible. And the program was stellar.

And dammit, it wasn't all *that* near to Cal so it wouldn't matter if things really were over between them. He'd be on the base, where she couldn't go, or traipsing around the world. Chances of her running into him would be slim. And if she did, she'd just make sure she looked as if she were living her best life to show him what he'd given up.

She'd spent those last one hundred and seventy-two days a slave to her phone. Checking it was charged and had signal obsessively. Bringing it to the bathroom with her. Setting the ringer to as loud as possible so she'd hear it if he called and she was asleep.

By day seven she hated even the sight of her cell phone. Even so, she didn't have it in her to turn it off so she left it there, on the side, while she did the bravest thing she'd possibly ever done. She emailed the admissions office and requested a tour of the campus of Southern California University.

After she got all the information and had even priced flights, she was so excited, she jumped up and ran downstairs to tell Myra. Halfway down the staircase she realized she'd forgotten her phone up in her room and this time she didn't go back for it.

CHAPTER THIRTY-FIVE

A week.

Seven fucking days.

That's how long this in and out mission had taken. Which wouldn't have been a problem if Cal's mind had been in the game, instead of at home.

They'd been on a complete and total lockdown in the border country from where they'd staged their infiltration. No one could know a team of US Navy SEALs were stuck there cooling their heels until command decided it was safe to move in and grab the target.

No calls. No internet. No leaving the safe house. Nothing but foreign television and high-strung nerves among the team as they waited.

Sit around and wait. That should be the SEAL motto

and Cal should have been used to it by now. That fact was no consolation after the long and frustrating week and equally long and frustrating journey home.

He didn't even have his cell phone—it was locked in his cage on base—so when the transport began its descent he still couldn't power it on and send a text to Pru.

But it was all finally coming to an end. The finish line was in sight. The target had been acquired and turned over to the proper authorities. And as the wheels of the transport touched down at Coronado, Cal was finally home.

Hmm. *Home* didn't feel like the right word anymore. Especially as he made a beeline to his cage and the cell phone he'd left there. He powered it on so he could call his real home in New York—which was another thought he hadn't had in many, many years.

He pushed aside the internal *where is home* debate and waited for the cell to do its thing. Texts loaded. Voicemails too. But before reading a single text or listening to even one voicemail, what he did first was tap Pru's name in his contact list and wait for the call to connect.

The fact there was no answer and, after too many unanswered rings, the call went to her voicemail had him in a panic. He skimmed the text messages and didn't see anything urgent. He also didn't see anything recent. They were all days old and that was concerning.

Cal's next call was to Apalachin. If there was anything happening, the crew there would know.

"Calvin," Vincent said instead of hello.

"Vincent," Cal returned. "I just got back and I can't reach Pru. What's happening there? Is everyone all right?"

"Everything's fine as far as I know. At least it was an hour ago."

"How do you know?" Cal demanded.

"I, uh, spoke to Myra."

Cal's brows shot up. But his grandmother's love life was a discussion for another time as Vincent continued. "I do have updates for you. We have an ID on the body at the warehouse."

"And?"

"He was the guy who owned the Narcan vending machines," Vincent revealed.

Not really a surprise. "He wasn't working alone," Cal reminded. "We know that at least two people were responsible for the kidnappings."

"You're right. He wasn't. Trust me, that was obvious when he approached us about the machine for Apalachin that he wasn't the brains of the operation."

"So who was?" Cal asked.

"A little digging yielded he was working with an inspector. An inspector who, for a cut of the take, would look the other way and not report that—and this is also something we discovered after you'd left— he was selling a Chinese counterfeit product as real Narcan for the full name-brand price."

"In machines that were supposed to be distributing it for free, according to the terms of the government grant they received to buy the real product for distribution," Cal added. "Do we have to worry about the inspector talking to the cops? They might bring him in for questioning if the authorities can put it all together."

Cal remembered the whopper of a lie he'd told the police and how he'd basically pinned the death of the machines' owner on him. The inspector would definitely rather talk than go down for murder.

"No, we don't have to worry," Vincent said.

Cal was afraid to ask how Vincent knew that with such certainty for fear he'd find out the body count had just doubled.

"I know what you're thinking, and no, we didn't strong arm him or do anything else… permanent. He was smart enough to see the light. And take an early retirement. That was Myra's influence, by the way."

"Grandmother? How?"

"She was dead set on reporting the scam to that grant agency. I told the inspector he was going down. He'd definitely do time for his part in all of it. The kidnapping. The counterfeit product from China he was rubber stamping as legit Narcan. Or he could keep his mouth shut, take an early retirement and disappear. He chose wisely."

"And Grandmother?"

"All she knows is that the shell company she reported is now officially closed. Out of business. The road's clear for her to get the grant and set up those machines the right way. Distributing the product for free."

Wow. A lot had happened in a week. And all without Cal's assistance. Maybe his family didn't need him there to protect them after all. That bristled but was also a relief. As long as his life was split in two—half belonging to the Navy and the other half to his family, it was nice to know he had backup from his unofficial team in Apalachin.

"Vincent, I don't know how to thank you."

"Already told you. I'll figure out a way."

Cal laughed. "I know you will. Bye, Vincent."

"Goodbye, son."

Feeling better, he navigated to his contacts list.

He'd try Pru one more time and if she still didn't answer, he'd move on to Cadence. He wouldn't feel one-hundred percent confident things were okay until he heard it from them directly.

Before he could implement his plan, the cell vibrated in his hand and Pru's name appeared on the display.

He tapped the call. "Pru. Hi. I called you. There was no answer. I was worried."

She let out a laugh that sounded almost like a sob. "You were worried?"

"You okay?"

"Yes."

"I don't believe you. I'm so sorry. I never thought we'd be gone that long. I swear it was supposed to be in and out—" Her sniff cut off anything more he was going to say.

"It's okay," she said with a definite wobble in her voice.

"It's not okay. But we'll figure it out. All right? It might be rough as we both find our footing but I swear to you, we'll make it work. I want to make this work."

She was definitely crying. He heard her stuttering intake of breath. "Okay." Her voice shook as she said the word.

"Do you want me to call back later—"

"No. Don't hang up."

"I won't. Promise." He'd scared her being gone so long. Hopefully she'd get used to his being away or the life of a team girlfriend was going to be tough on her. "Tell me what you've been doing this past week."

"Well, I kind of did something crazy."

He didn't love the sound of that. That statement from his sister would have him assuming she'd gone on a shopping spree. But from his always practical Pru—he couldn't even imagine what she'd done.

Cal tried to sound casual as he said, "Oh, yeah? What did you do?"

"I made an appointment to take a campus tour. I'm thinking of going back to school."

"That's great. Where?" he asked. It would be nice if she could go to Cornell with Cadence. Then she'd have a built-in support system.

"Um, don't be mad…" she began.

"Why would I be mad?" he asked, frowning.

"The school's in southern California."

Sometimes he wanted to shake some sense into his girl until she believed in him. In them. Her faith in them would come with time, he hoped. For now, all he could do was try to make her believe in him.

"Why in the world would I be angry about that?" he asked.

"Well, because it's so close to you. You'd really be okay with me being there?"

What was she talking about? His crazy girl. Could she really think he'd ever not want to see her?

"I can't think of anything better than you being here close to me." He'd say it as often as he had to, to make her believe it.

"Okay. I'm not even sure I'll be accepted so—"

"You'll be accepted," he assured her. "When are you coming? How soon?"

"Next week. Do you think you'll be around?"

"I have every intention of being here. I'll pick you up at the airport. You can stay at my place." He'd request leave for those days to insure he was there when she was.

"I'd like that."

He heard the smile in her voice and matched it with one of his own. *I love you* almost slipped out of his mouth. He held it back. He could wait a week. That would be something best said in person.

"Oh, I almost forgot to tell you. Myra got a flower delivery from Vincent! It was so big the florist sent two people to wrestle it into the house."

What the fuck? Cal coughed on his surprise. "Wow. That's...interesting."

She laughed. "That's what I thought. About as interesting as Myra asking me to teach her how to text."

"Jeezus," Cal ran a hand over his face and tried not to picture any geriatric sexting that might be happening between those two back at his other home, with the other people he loved. "You know, when you're at school here we can fly home to New York together for the holidays," he said.

"You'd do that?" she asked.

"I'll certainly try." Just the thought of Christmas in front of the fire in New York with Pru and Cadence and his grandmother—even his father—had him grinning. "I'll put in for leave over Christmas today."

"That would be nice."

"Sweetheart, things are going to be way more than just *nice* between us once you're living out here."

"I can't wait."

Neither could he.

And just like that, the idea of Pru moving to California made it seem like home again, just like New York was his home. *Home* was where ever the people he loved were. It was as simple as that.

EPILOGUE

"When are you going to let me see where you're taking me?" Pru asked, tired of wearing the eye mask even if it was silk and had been a gift from Cadence for her cross country flight. That and a new sketchbook and pencils.

Pru was starting classes at The University of Southern California in a week. She'd be living on campus once the semester started since it was two hours from Coronado, but she was spending the next few days with Cal at his place. Which she'd seen when she'd been there for the campus tour so she didn't understand his making her cover her eyes now.

"We're almost there."

She pouted. "Fine."

Finally, she felt him shift the Bronco into gear. Cal

had purchased himself the new version of the SUV. It was what he drove in California. She wasn't surprised by that at all, given how much he loved his old Bronco back in New York.

"Okay, you can take off the mask now."

She did and the first thing she saw with her slightly blurred vision was his smiling face. That was before her focus moved past him and to the beach house in front of her. "Did you rent a beach house for the week for us?"

"Nope." He shook his head, his smile growing wider.

She narrowed her eyes. "Cal. What did you do?"

"I remembered that I too have a trust fund. And that I hadn't touched it. Not even once. All that stubbornness on my part allowed it to grow. Pretty big, it turns out. So I bought a beach house."

"You what? You're crazy!"

"Not really. I was renting before, which really was crazy, if you know rents in Coronado. This is actually going to save me money. And I can always sell it when I retire if I want to move back to New York. Or hell, keep it and become a landlord." He shrugged. "But until then, it's ours for when you visit."

He released his seatbelt and opened the door.

Glancing back at her, still frozen with shock, he said, "Come on. I wanna show you inside."

"Okay." She finally got her legs moving and followed him.

It got more beautiful the closer she got. The view. The patio, complete with grill and hammock. The fire pit with the circle of chairs around it.

And inside—it was bright and airy and modern. Everything that the house in New York wasn't. The kitchen was open to the vaulted-ceilinged living room with the wall of windows facing the water and the large screen television on a wall above the gas fireplace.

"Cal. It's amazing."

"There's more." He grabbed her hand and pulled her through a doorway. "This is your study."

"My study?" she repeated, unable to comprehend what he was saying while faced with the floor to ceiling library shelves that took up one entire wall. The top shelves accessible by an actual sliding library ladder.

He nodded. "So you can do your school work while you're here."

School work. Forget school work. She had enough room to create her own library. Complete with a ladder. "Cal. The shelves."

It was all she could get out of her mouth as she still stood staring in awe.

"I thought you might like those." He stepped up behind her and wrapped his arms around her waist from the back. "You going to be able to fill all these?"

"Just watch me." She turned in his arms and said, "Thank you." Then she showed him her thanks, rising up onto her toes and reaching for his mouth.

He kissed her long and hard, then pulled away. "That brings us to the next stop on the tour."

"The bedroom?" she asked hopefully.

"Smart girl." He grinned.

Her joy over the pillow strewn king sized bed was only surpassed by the view from the second-floor bedroom that opened to a private balcony via double French doors.

"I don't know what to say." She shook her head.

"Well you'd better think of something. Because there's one last surprise." He flipped on the television in the bedroom and she wondered if he was about to show her all his streaming channels or something.

But what came on screen was better than HBO. Cadence, Myra, and even Peanut stood in the living room of the big house. "What? What is this?" she asked.

"I have video chat hooked up to both of the

televisions in the house, so you can see everyone in New York whenever you want. Or we can chat while I'm deployed." Cal smiled wickedly.

That last suggestion had her cheeks heating as why the video chat was on the bedroom television as well as the living room.

"Do you love it?" Cadence asked. "We knew about it for weeks and had to keep quiet."

"It was very difficult for some of us," Myra added, shooting a glance at Cadence.

"You're the one who almost slipped the other day, Grandmother," Cadence accused.

"Now, girls. Don't argue." Vincent walked into view and Pru's eyes widened. She glanced at Cal and saw he was just as surprised as she was.

"Hello, Vincent," Cal managed to say.

"Hello, son. Your girl like your surprise?"

"She loved it."

Vincent nodded then turned to the two women in the room. "We might want to cut this call short and give them some privacy. A house like that is going to require a lot of christening.

Myra actually giggled, which might be the biggest shock of Pru's day.

"Talk later. Text me!" Cadence said as she flipped the lid of her laptop closed.

Pru turned to Cal.

"Overwhelmed?" he asked.

"A little bit."

"Want a drink?"

"Mm. Eventually." She took a step closer and rested her hands on his chest.

He took a step forward, closing the remaining distance between them. "Want to try out that bed?"

"Definitely."

"I was hoping you'd say that." He bracketed her face between his palms and asked, "Do you know how much I love you?"

She was starting to. And if she thought about it too much she'd cry, so she said, "Not as much as I love you."

Cal narrowed his eyes. "We'll debate about that. Later."

He grabbed her hand and tugged her toward the bed as she said, "Much later."

Glancing back at her, he grinned. "Like I said. Smart girl."

THE LONG ROAD HOME COLLECTION
from the Binge Read Babes

My Heart's Home Kris Michaels
Home to Stay Maryann Jordan
Finding Home Abbie Zanders
Home Again Caitlyn O'Leary
Home Front Cat Johnson

Searching for Home Kris Michaels
Home Port Maryann Jordan
Home Base Abbie Zanders
Home Fires Cat Johnson
Defending Home Caitlyn O'Leary

ABOUT THE AUTHOR

A New York Times and USA Today bestselling author, Cat Johnson writes contemporary romance featuring sexy alpha heroes, who sometimes wear cowboy or combat boots, and the sassy heroines brave enough to love them. Known for her creative marketing, Cat has sponsored bull-riding cowboys, used bologna to promote her romance novels, and owns a collection of camouflage and cowboy boots for book signings. She writes both full-length and shorter works available in eBook, paperback and audiobook.

For more visit CatJohnson.net
Get new release and deal alerts at
CatJohnson.net/news

Printed in Great Britain
by Amazon

38582736R10184